MW01709406

Tarte Tatin Murder

A Seagrass Sweets Cozy Mystery

Book 2

Sandi Scott

Cover design by Megan Theodoro.

GRATICE PRESS

Table of Contents

Note to the Reader

If you would like recipes for many of the sweet treats that Ashley is baking in this book, you can find them on my website here:

www.SandiScottBooks.com/recipes

CHAPTER 1

"Merciful macaroons!" exclaimed Ashley, slamming on the brakes and barely missing the man in a CURE Cancer T-shirt and an absurd straw hat that covered his forehead down to his eyes. He waved vaguely in her direction as he zoomed away, the piles of sponsorship signs in his cart so high that he couldn't actually see her. Dust shrouded several people walking across the lot as the cart zipped past them, too fast and too close for the crowd.

Still grumbling about the cart driver's carelessness, Ashley looked around the parking lot for more hazards. The other volunteers scurried about the lot, taking care of last-minute details for the non-profit cancer research foundation's golfing fundraiser. She had parked her van as close to the clubhouse as possible and jumped out to open the back just before she was almost mowed down by the reckless cart driver.

One of the volunteers waved and shouted, "Are you okay? That guy's a menace with all those signs piled on top of the ice chests and that stupid hat blocking his vision. He didn't even stop to make sure you were all right; so rude!"

Ashley waved back. "Yeah, I'm fine; he just startled me. With this many people milling around in the parking lot, I can't believe he'd be that careless; some of them aren't moving nearly fast enough to get out of his way in time. It would be a pretty depressing start to the tournament for someone to be hurt before they even got inside the club. Anyway, it looks like a good turnout of helpers today."

The volunteer reached the back of Ashley's van. "For sure—it looks like we'll have plenty of people to cover things for once. Speaking of covering, I'd better hustle my bustle. I'm supposed to be checking in the golfers starting in three minutes, and those old goats get testy if you make them wait. The sooner they get started, the sooner they can get back to the bar and that's the only reason some of them play golf in the first place."

Chuckling, Ashley paused to admire the landscaping at the front of the club—red and orange double hibiscus, yellow esperanza and blue plumbago showcasing an iron picket fence with an arched gate twined with butterfly vine, its unique seed pods looking like butterflies hovering. Picking up a tray of scrumptious French pastries, she headed for the rather plain wood and cinder block building and tugged open the heavy, ornately carved door. Her eyes widened as she took in the opulence of the place—marble floors, gilded wall sconces, crystal chandeliers, heavy velvet drapes. "I don't think we're in Kansas anymore, Toto—or in little ol' Seagrass, Texas, either! I don't know whether to be impressed or appalled!" As she turned in circles, lost in taking in the spectacle, she didn't notice any of the people wandering around her, their voices fading into a vague murmur.

She jumped as a deep voice said, "Welcome to the Seagrass Country Club!" Turning, she saw a young man, decked out in a formal business suit, standing at a small carved cherry wood desk just inside the door. "How may I assist you today?"

"My name is Ashley Adams; I'm the dessert caterer for the CURE fundraiser. Where should I set up the food?"

"If you will follow me, I'll escort you to the banquet room. The foundation is using that room during the day for light refreshments before the awards ceremony this evening. Do you need assistance unloading your desserts?"

Ashley wasn't about to turn down the offer. "That would be great. It's pretty warm out there today, so getting the chocolates inside as quickly as possible is probably a good idea!"

The young man pulled a small walkie-talkie from inside his jacket. "Hank, please come to the banquet room to assist the caterer." A short blast of static followed, and the young man continued, "Hank should be here in just a moment; if you'll excuse me, I'll get back to directing incoming traffic. Some of our members feel neglected if someone isn't there to call them by name as soon as they walk in the door."

Another young man stepped around the corner, this one in dress slacks and a short-sleeved shirt embroidered with the country club logo on the pocket. He grinned at her as he held his hand out to shake hers.

"Hi! I'm Hank. Greg said you needed some help carrying something?"

"Hank, thanks! I'm Ashley, and I have

pastries and chocolates to bring in for the CURE fundraiser. I definitely appreciate your offer to help!"

"Oh, yum—that sounds good! We'd better get them in quickly; we wouldn't want them to melt before the golfers get to taste them. They can sometimes be a bit fussy!"

As Hank and Ashley returned to the clubhouse with the next load, Hank commented, "I noticed you looking at all the glitz—pretty over the top, huh?" Clearly, he'd seen the same reaction before and found it amusing.

Ashley laughed. "I can't decide if it's beautifully sophisticated or if it's really cheesy and tasteless! It's hard to imagine that something this sumptuous is in little Seagrass! And you certainly don't expect anything like it when you see the outside. I know the merchants' association has been pretty successful in getting a more well-heeled type of tourist, but this has been here longer than that, hasn't it? And old Seagrass screams beach shack and barbecue joint. The décor here just doesn't fit that image."

"Some things don't change," Hank replied. "There have always been people with more money than common sense, and folks who saw the need to show off that money. The club has been around since the early 1920s, but it wasn't 'old money' that built it. The original members were definitely nouveau riche, and pretty snobbish about it! We read some of their journals and the newspaper accounts of the opening and events in my local history class. It was pretty obvious that cliques and arrogance aren't just a modern invention."

Since moving back to her hometown of Seagrass, Ashley was often surprised to discover places she had never known as a child or teenager living with her parents. It was always a delight to feel like a visitor in her hometown.

The last trays and boxes set on the table, Ashley thanked her helper and handed him a cream-filled mini profiterole. "Here, take a pastry with you."

The high-nineties temperature and 83 percent humidity had made carting in the miniature eclairs, stacks of hazelnut and chocolate crepes, and bite-sized *tarte tatin* squares hot work. Before she started arranging the pastries on silver serving trays, she stepped over to the bar, looking for a glass of water.

"Please tell me you are here with my liquor order," the bartender, a petite blonde, begged. "As you can see, this bar is almost dry, and that won't do at all. The CURE guys are hoping for a big take on the fundraiser, and folks always bid higher at silent auctions when they're a bit lubricated beforehand."

"Sorry, I'm just the dessert caterer; I can't help you with the alcohol thing at all. I was hoping I could get a glass of water to cool off while I finish setting up. My name is Ashley; I own Seagrass Sweets, the catering company.

"Geez, I'm sorry!" was the reply, "The supplier said the delivery's on the way; it should have been here yesterday, but he said the order had never been placed. He thought he could get it here two hours ago, but I haven't seen any sign of the truck or the booze. I guess I'm freaking a little. Some of the members are already grousing about having to wait for their first drinks."

Ashley glanced at her watch. "Really? It's not even ten o'clock in the morning! Are they really looking for alcohol this early?"

"I guess some of them prefer hooch to hot coffee; we had to start locking up the stuff because a few of the members would help themselves to drinks before we open up at eight most mornings." She scooped ice into a large glass and filled it with water, then handed it to Ashley. "I'm Stacey. Just let me know if you need anything from the bar. It's going to be a long day for both of us!"

Carrying her drink back to the dessert table, Ashley covered the serving tables with the vintage tablecloths she'd inherited from her great-grandmother, tone-on-tone flowers and vines embellishing a light ivory linen background. She used dainty pastel-stitched lady's handkerchiefs in place of a runner to add a subtle touch of color. With the antique tiered porcelain dishes and engraved silver trays, the table was elegant but still exuded warmth, a "high society meets country chic" effect that didn't take itself too seriously. The effect was subtle enough to accent the food without distracting from it, and Ashley felt a twinge of pride as she surveyed the display. She knew Great-grandmother Estelle would approve of the way Ashley was using the heirlooms and that she would be proud of her great-granddaughter's business, especially because at least half of the recipes were from the handwritten cookbooks Ashley had inherited from her.

As she arranged eclairs, cream puffs, and

slices of opera cake on the tiers and filled the crepes with chocolate-hazelnut spread and raspberries before dusting them with powdered sugar, an attractive silver-haired man wearing a CURE polo shirt and plaid golfing slacks walked up. His moss-green eyes twinkled, implying a friendly, charming personality with a hint of mischief lurking inside and giving Ashley the impression of a slightly naughty young boy hiding in a grown-up body. She wondered briefly what he'd been like as a child.

"Hello, there—you must be Ashley! I'm Charles Brady, Ryan's uncle. After all the great things Ryan has told me about them, I can't wait to sample your desserts!"

Ashley smiled and offered him her hand. "I'm so glad to meet you, Mr. Brady. Ryan said that you would be here today. He used to mention you occasionally when we worked together at SmithCorp. He always told me that you were just like a father to him."

"Oh, I know you worked together; Ryan's told me a lot about you, and not just about your baking!" Ashley blushed a little, wondering what exactly Ryan had told his uncle; she had a hard time just trying to figure out what Ryan thought of her. "I have to say, though, his catering recommendation made one part of this crazy event simple for the planning committee." He winked at Ashley, making her blush even more.

Ryan and she reconnected when she first moved back to Seagrass, picking up where they left off as chummy, flirtatious coworkers. Then, when a crazy turn of events had Ashley investigating a murder, Ryan had been a tremendous help to her. They had spent so much time working the mystery together that she started to remember why some mornings during her time working that dead-end tech services job at SmithCorp, he was the only reason she looked forward to going to work. After they solved the mystery, Ryan asked her out to dinner and she accepted, although she was nervous about taking their friendship to the next level. But then he had to travel for several weeks for one of his biggest clients at his I.T. consulting firm and they still hadn't found a time for their dinner date. Ashley still wanted to go, maybe now more than ever, but they hadn't talked about it for almost a week. She was afraid Ryan regretted asking her and now she wasn't sure if Ryan was interested now in anything more than a friendship. Maybe Uncle Charlie would drop a clue or two.

"It's a good thing I was a Boy Scout growing up," he said, tapping the etched silver flask tucked into his breast pocket and nodding toward the bar. "I came prepared for an emergency, and it looks like we have one over there—not a drop of Scotch whiskey in the place. What kind of bar has no alcohol on hand?" Based on the way he listed slightly to the side, Ashley suspected he'd already broached his emergency stash more than once that morning.

Before she could respond, a yelp from the silent auction tables startled them. They turned to see an older, distinguished-looking man pretending to brush non-existent crumbs off the front of a pretty young brunette's blouse. He had her trapped between two tables, leaning close and leering, and her eyes were flitting around desperately, looking for an escape route.

"Ah, yes," Charlie remarked. "My golf partner for the day, the brilliant Oliver Green, genius researcher and self-proclaimed gift to women, has already begun his play. He's closer to finding a cure for cancer than anyone else in the world, but he rather lacks the social skills necessary to charm women—or anyone else, for that matter."

As they watched, the couple's interactions became more and more awkward. The woman's body language said clearly that she wasn't interested in his advances but didn't know how to reject them without offense, and she kept trying to find a way to move away from him. Green, however, was totally unaware that she was repulsed rather than intrigued, and he kept sliding closer and closer, clearly ignoring polite society's usual personal boundaries.

"Excuse me, Ashley. I'd better go rescue our lovely volunteer before she either faints dead away or screams for her lawyer to sue us. It was a pleasure to finally meet you, and I look forward to getting to know you better." Charlie touched Ashley warmly on the shoulder as he walked over to Green, slapping him on the back and starting a conversation, giving the grateful volunteer a chance to escape.

Ashley pulled out her phone and quickly texted Ryan.

"*Thx tons for job referral. Just met ur uncle –great guy*!"

Her phone beeped seconds later.

"*Beware crazy Uncle Charlie. There's no telling what wild things he'll get up to!*"

CHAPTER 2

Tucking her phone back into the pocket of her black-and-white checked chef's trousers, Ashley checked to be sure there were no empty spaces on the dessert table, then glanced around the room. Everyone except a few volunteers had left for the golf course, leaving her with a bit of time to herself to look at the other tables. As she looked through the silent auction items, she found the "Private Chef Experience with the world-renowned Patty LaFontaine" gift certificate, and was delighted to see that the bid was already up to $1,000. Patty would be thrilled to know that her donation was a hit. If she served *Les Desserts Français*' *tarte tatin* and bonbons, as she planned, it would be great for Ashley as well.

"Next year," Ashley mused, "I should make a donation, too. Maybe I could offer a dessert-of-the-month subscription for a year's worth of desserts. Or maybe a brunch or afternoon tea for four." She found a couple of items that interested her, but the bids were already way above her budget.

The tables also included photographs and brief biographies for each of the CURE board members and the researchers. Oliver Green's showed he was considered one of the leading cancer researchers at the University of Houston and credited with major advances in the field of drug treatment for cancer. According to his profile, his current project, housed at the university's nearby Victoria campus, had shown very promising results during the clinical trials and was on the fast-track for FDA approval. Ashley noticed that his partner in the project, Dr. Wendy Graham, was an attractive and fairly young woman.

Ashley drifted back to the dessert table and fussed with the display, then pulled out her phone and found the mystery e-book she'd started reading the night before. She settled back into her chair and let herself get caught up in the amateur gumshoe's adventures. Eventually golfers began trickling back in, hot from the South Texas sun, and either celebrating or sulking over the results of their golf rounds. They collected petit fours, mini croissants stuffed with fresh strawberries and whipped cream, rich opera cake, and chocolate-covered bonbons as they updated their bids on the silent auction items. Apparently the liquor order had arrived; most of them carried half-filled glasses, and everyone seemed to be in good spirits. A few people wandered over to the tables, chatting about their rounds and the latest town gossip.

"Last call for bids! Bidding will close in 15

minutes, folks, so make sure you've placed your best bids on the items you can't live without. Again, bidding will close in 15 minutes!"

As she listened to the auction chairperson's announcement, Ashley noticed a disturbance at the French doors leading in from the golf course. She looked up to see Charlie stumbling in, clearly and cheerily drunk as the proverbial skunk.

"Gotta 'mergency—gotta be prepared! Here to help—gonna take care of it," Charlie slurred as he leaned a bit too far forward and went lurching farther into the room. "No worries—got this one covered!"

Several club members looked in his direction and leaned together to whisper gleeful disapproval of his condition.

"Mr. Brady, I think you need to rest after your morning in the sun. Is there someone you can call to pick you up? You don't look like you feel well enough to be driving." It was the young man who'd greeted Ashley on her arrival. She was impressed by his tact in pretending to believe Charlie was suffering from overexposure to the sun rather than obvious booze consumption.

"'Course I do! Plentya friends—just pick one out and they'll be here! Now, where's that danged phone gotten to this time?" Charlie fumbled in his pockets, turning them out, but his phone was clearly missing. "Know I had it—'mergency call. Where's the 'mergency?"

"Uncle Charlie, let me get hold of Ryan; I'm sure he'll know of someone who can drive you home," Ashley said, texting Ryan as she spoke.

"No rush—gotta take care of the 'mergency first." Charlie continued patting his pockets. "Where's that stupid phone? Hate those things—never leave you alone."

"Uncle Charlie's crocked—needs a ride. Who 2 call?"

When Ryan replied that he'd be right there,

Ashley took Charlie's arm, steering him towards the bar. "Ryan's on his way. Why don't we wait for him here?" She signaled the bartender for coffee and asked, "How was your game? Did you do well?"

"Didn't finish, but it wouldn'ta mattered. Danged Oliver was beating me badly and being a horse's behind about it. I coulda killed him for rubbing my nose in it." Charlie continued grumbling under his breath.

"Why did you quit before you finished? Were you losing that badly?"

"Don't remember; had a 'mergency in the clubhouse." He looked at her blearily and reached for his flask. "'Mergency-only flask; came to fix the 'mergency, so it's the right place for it!" As he tipped the flask to swig the whiskey, Ashley noticed that it was still full enough that the contents sloshed down his shirt front. She wondered how he'd managed to get so drunk without emptying the flask. She might even has thought it *was* from the sun if not for the fumes rolling off him, the odor so strong that it was almost visible.

She tried to get him to drink the hot, black coffee Stacey brought over, but he was having none of it. He looked at the mug blearily and then pushed it away, hefting his flask once again.

"Stupid bar dry this morning; what good's a bar without booze? Good thing I have plenty friends to help," Charlie mumbled as he patted his "friend" and lifted it to his mouth again.

"Uncle Charlie, why don't we step out on the terrace for a little fresh air?" Ashley tried to guide him back toward the French doors, hoping to keep him from creating any more of a scene and giving the busybodies more grist for the gossip mill.

He refused to budge. "Got nothing left to do out there today, and it's too danged hot for anything human to move around. I'm staying right here. Not going back out there to sweat or to listen to that blowhard Green bragging about his golf score."

After what seemed like an hour, but was probably less than ten minutes, Ryan walked in, looking hot and cross. He glanced around until he saw them and then stomped over to where they sat.

"Uncle Charlie, what are you thinking? You're stinking drunk at an important public event. What's gotten into you lately? I don't think I've even seen you tipsy before, much less falling down drunk." Despite his obvious annoyance, Ryan clearly was worried about his favorite uncle.

"And what's going on outside?" he asked Ashley. "I haven't seen that many police cars in one place since the Memorial Day parade, and there's an ambulance out there, too. Someone get too hot or throw their clubs through a window because they lost a round?"

"Police cars? Really? I haven't heard anything," Ashley answered. "It must not have been too serious; we didn't hear any sirens—

didn't even know they were out there! No one has said anything in here, either, and there hasn't been any kind of a fuss that I noticed. Come to think of it, that *is* kind of strange."

"Well, let me get good-time Charlie here to the car, so I can pour him into bed. Man, is he going to have a sore head in the morning! And it looks like he's sporting a pretty good sun-burn, too. I think I'll make sure to avoid him for a couple of days, until he remembers who he is again."

"Make sure he drinks plenty of water be-fore he sleeps," Ashley suggested, "and leave a bottle of water next to his bed. That will help the hangover some, anyway. Do you want some help getting him home?"

"Nah, if you'll help me get him moving, I can take it from there. I used to have to get my roommates settled after their binge-drinking parties. I know how to handle him."

Together, they got Charlie standing and walked him to the door. Charlie's car was parked in the first row, so Ryan took his uncle's keys, making Ashley raise an eyebrow.

“I’ll come back later for my car,” Ryan explained. “I had to park on the street about two blocks from the entrance thanks to all the emergency vehicles blocking the entrance to the lot.” As they leaned Charlie against the back door so that Ryan could unlock the car, two uniformed sheriff's deputies approached them, looking grim.

"One of you Charles Brady?" asked the pudgy, gray-haired deputy.

"Yeah, that's me. Who wants to know?"

"You were Oliver Green's golf partner today?"

"Yeah, I got stuck with that loud-mouthed old fool. So what?" Charlie was reaching the belligerent drunk stage rapidly. "I shoulda killed him for being such a jerk. He had the nerve to ask me for money while lording it over me that he was beating me at golf, like that was such a big deal. "

"You need to come with us, sir. Got some questions for you," said the other deputy, a redhead who didn't look old enough to be out of high school, much less the police academy. He looked nervous, as if he didn't really know what to do if Charlie decided not to cooperate.

"Sean, I know he's drunk, but I can get him home," Ryan insisted, stepping in front of Charlie while keeping a hand on him to prevent him from toppling over. "He didn't cause any trouble; we got him outside without a scene. Surely you don't have to arrest him if I just get him away from here now."

"Son," the older deputy responded, "this is a mite more serious than public intoxication. He's going to have to come to the station and answer some questions."

Charlie continued muttering, "Somebody ought to shut that guy up."

"Station? Questions? About what?" Ryan looked puzzled.

The younger cop took Charlie's arm and

started pulling him toward a patrol car. Ryan's uncle tried to jerk away, stumbling and lurching as he overbalanced.

"Hey, hands off, youngster—show some 'spect for your elders," Charlie snarled. "Go way—don't wanna talk 'bout that jerk anymore. Never gonna spend time with him again."

The other deputy glanced over at his partner and Charlie, then turned back to answer Ryan. "It seems that someone did shut Oliver Green up—permanently. He's been murdered, and your uncle is our number one suspect. He's going to have a lot of explaining to do before he goes home again. You can meet us at the station if you want."

Stunned, Ashley and Ryan watched the deputies tuck Charlie into the patrol car. He was still fighting them and muttering about Green. Ryan called out, "Uncle, I'll meet you at the station," just as the door slammed and the deputies drove away.

He looked at Ashley, panic in his eyes. "I can't believe this! Ash, there's no way Uncle Charlie killed anyone. I know he's sozzled, but he's not a killer. In fact, I don't think he could stand up long enough to kill anyone. This looks bad, but I know him. I know he wouldn't kill someone, especially not over a golf game."

"Go to the station and find out what's going on. I'll pack up and call you when I get home. If you need me before then, call my cell. It's going to work out; it will be okay." Ashley gave Ryan a little push toward the car and then hurried back inside to gather her belongings.

CHAPTER 3

Looking back to be sure she hadn't left anything behind on or under the tables, Ashley hit a solid wall of uniform. She looked up into a tanned face with a scruffy five o'clock shadow, and said, "Oof! Oh, Sheriff Mueller, I'm sorry! I guess I should have been watching where I'm going instead of where I've already been!"

The sheriff chuckled. "No harm done! I should have been paying more attention, too. How have you been, Ashley?"

"Busy, busy, busy—and that's just the way I like it!" After a second, Ashley's smile dimmed. "Sheriff, what happened out there today? Was it really murder? And do you *really* think Charlie Brady had anything to do with it?"

The sheriff hesitated, looking over her head. "Well, I really shouldn't tell you anything about an on-going investigation." He held up his hand as she started to protest. "Hold on—I said I *shouldn't*, not that I won't! I can't tell you everything, but, since you've been such a help in the past, I can give you a bit of information. You'll hear it all through the grapevine in another hour, anyway."

Ashley laughed. "What on earth is going on in town that you think it will take that long? I'm surprised I haven't already gotten five or six calls—with all the wrong details!"

"Yeah, you're probably right. Anyway, it looks to me like things got a bit too heated—no pun intended—and ol' Charlie bopped Green on the head; my investigators tell me the preliminary cause of death looks to be blunt force trauma. Of course, under Texas law, we'll have to have an autopsy, since this was an unattended death, but my guys don't miss many!"

"Who found him? And why are you so sure it was Charlie who hit him?"

"A golf twosome found him in the rough at the seventh hole; the body had been shoved under some leaves in the underbrush. As for Charlie—well, he was Green's partner, he was drunk, and he disappeared off the greens for no reason that we can find. I'm pretty sure that a blood and DNA analysis of his bag and clubs will give us everything we need to wrap this up. It's too bad; Charlie Brady's a good man, and it's sad that booze pushed him over the edge. He'd never even have thought of hurting someone if he'd been sober."

Ashley pondered for a second and then asked, "But, Sheriff, if he'd just killed someone, why would he come back to the clubhouse? Why not just leave? I sat with him at the bar for at least ten minutes while we waited for Ryan to pick him up. He could have gotten a fair distance from the club in that time, especially if he'd left the course a while before that."

Mueller looked at her and shook his head. "Hon, he was stewed to the gills. I doubt he even knew that he was in the clubhouse. Did he say anything strange?"

She decided to leave out Charlie's comment that he could have killed his partner, knowing that he'd incriminated himself enough with his comments to the deputies. "Just that he had a flask in his pocket 'for emergencies.' He was pretty well-oiled; he couldn't find his phone. But he didn't say anything that sounded like he'd just bashed someone over the head with a golf club. And, like Ryan said, I don't think he could stand up straight enough to hit someone with anything, much less a golf club, without falling over himself, especially not hard enough to kill.

And Charlie didn't have any scratches or debris to show he'd fallen."

"Well, drunks can pull some pretty dumb stunts, and it will surprise you what they're capable of when you think they're seconds from passing out. Right now, though, I'd better get back inside and see what else the detectives have found out, and then I have to head back to the station. My wife is not going to be happy that I won't be home for supper; her sister and brother-in-law are supposed to be there—not that I mind missing that part! See you soon, under better circumstances, I hope!"

He started to walk away and then turned back, his face serious. "Ashley, leave this one alone. Do not get involved in investigating; we have our killer—we'll close it up shortly."

Ashley didn't bother to respond. She didn't agree with the sheriff's assumptions, but she knew that she didn't have anything that would convince him—yet.

As she slid the last box into the back of her van, she realized that she'd left her portable crepe maker in the kitchen. Since she'd need it for tomorrow's afternoon tea event, she went back to the clubhouse. She headed to the kitchen where she'd had the unit plugged in, but the door was locked, and no one responded when she knocked. Looking around, she saw that the bartender was still around.

"Hey, Stacey, I left something in the kitchen; is there any chance you could let me in to get it?" She smiled, hoping a friendly face would help her convince the perky young woman to take pity and unlock the door.

"Nope, sorry; only Javier, the manager, has a key. Nobody gets into the kitchen without him knowing about it, ever since they caught a couple of the members making sandwiches from some fancy food bought for a special event."

"Do you know where I can find him?" Ashley smiled at her mental picture of some tipsy men demolishing elaborate banquet dishes. It wouldn't be funny if she was the caterer, but it did make her laugh to realize that raiding the refrigerator crossed social lines.

"Hell if I know; he disappeared early this morning, before the bigwigs starting showing up. One of the biggest events we've had this year, and he bails, leaving me with a dry bar because someone screwed up the inventory and didn't order enough booze—and he's the one who is responsible for making sure we're stocked up. I spent most of the day listening to members whining about not having their drinks or threatening to have me fired if I didn't pour booze I didn't have. Then, on top of that, there's this whole murder thing. I know Javier's been distracted lately, but, when we've got all these VIPs around, he could at least pretend to give a damn about his job and stick around where he's supposed to be. Ordering inventory and patting members on the head is above my pay grade, and it would be great if that guy would do his job and earn that higher paycheck."

"Um, well, thanks anyway," Ashley stammered, a little taken aback by the bartender's vehemence. "I guess I'll have to swing by tomorrow to get the rest of my things."

Shaking her head, Ashley crawled into the driver's seat of the catering van and pulled out her phone to call Ryan, but the call went straight to voice mail. She headed out, thinking that she'd try calling again when she got back to the commercial kitchen she and Patty shared.

CHAPTER 4

"Patty? Are you here?" Ashley pushed open the door to the kitchen with her box and dropped it on the stainless steel prep table. "Patty?"

"I guess I'm here alone," she thought. "I haven't seen Patty since—wow, I can't even remember!" Her friend had been a bit distant the last few weeks. It almost seemed like Patty was avoiding her, like she was hiding something. "Maybe I should call her and suggest a girls' night out." As she reached for her phone, it started to ring; the screen showed Ryan's number.

"Are you okay? How's Charlie?" she asked.

A deep sigh on the other end. "He's still at the station. They say that he won't see the justice of the peace or the judge before tomorrow, so he'll have to stay at the jail overnight. Sheriff Mueller is talking about taking him to the hospital first, though; he's worried about how drunk Uncle Charlie is. He wants the doctor to take a look and be sure he doesn't need some kind of treatment. I can't ever remember seeing anyone that drunk before. He blew almost three times the legal limit."

"Oh, Ryan! I'm so sorry! Is there anything I can do to help?"

"I don't know, Ash; I really don't know. Uncle Charlie is innocent—I'm sure of that. He's been like a second father to me all my life, and there is no way he'd kill someone over a golf game. I mean, I know he isn't perfect, and he's drinking way too much, but—he and Aunt Mercy are in the middle of a divorce, and it's turned really ugly and expensive. He still loves her and doesn't want the divorce, but she's got some other guy in the wings and wants all the money and property. I know it's not an excuse, but he's a harmless drunk. In fact, he usually doesn't touch alcohol anywhere but at home. He wouldn't intentionally hurt anyone, much less kill them, and definitely not over golf. I mean, he enjoys the game, but he doesn't care enough to get that mad over it!"

Ryan paused and then, voice quivering, said, "Ash, I need your help. I have to prove that Charlie's innocent. I can't let him go to prison for something I know he didn't do. I owe him so much; I have to help him."

"Let the police handle it, Ryan; that's their job. If Charlie's innocent—and I'm sure you're right that he is—they'll figure it out." Ashley could hear the doubt in her own voice, but she hoped Ryan couldn't.

"Oh, sure—they'll solve it easily, since they aren't even looking for any other possible suspects. They've decided it had to be my uncle, so they aren't even talking to—or about—anyone else. But that's not the truth, and my uncle is going to be railroaded into prison if I don't find a way to prove they're wrong."

Her turn to sigh. "Okay, take it easy; if we're going to help, you have to stay calm and in control of yourself. And yeah, I do know how hard that is—I do remember." She thought about how panicked she was when it looked like she would end up in prison for her ex-boyfriend's fraud and thefts. She was eventually able to prove her innocence—her naiveté, really—but it was a scary time, knowing that the police then were also convinced she was the guilty party. She paused, considering, and then continued, "I'll help you however I can. What do you already know about the case?"

"Nothing really; all they told me was that Oliver Green had been found dead on the golf course and that he had been murdered. Right about then, Charlie's attorney got to the station, and no one would tell me anything else. The attorney said he'd call me tomorrow, and Mueller told me to go home."

"Hmm. Well, I did find out that the cause of death was blunt force trauma, and Sheriff Mueller is having Charlie's golf clubs tested for blood and DNA. I think we're going to have to leave that part to them. I have to go back to the club in the morning, though, to pick up some stuff I left behind. I guess I can snoop around and see what I can learn there. I have to tell you, though—the only sure way to prove Charlie didn't kill Oliver is to find out who did. That could be dangerous, so we need to be careful."

She thought for a minute and then suggested, "Can you remotely access Charlie's phone to figure out where it is and then use GPS history to see where he was between the seventh hole and the clubhouse? If he wasn't with Green, we have to figure out where he was and if someone saw him there. He may not be able to remember any time soon, and I think it's going to be very important."

"I'm already on it. I should have it mapped out before too long."

Patty stepped into the kitchen, setting a box of kitchen gadgets on the stainless steel prep table, so Ashley said, "Listen, Patty just got here, I need to run. How about if we meet for breakfast tomorrow to compare notes? About nine, at the diner? That should give me enough time to snoop around the clubhouse a little, and maybe you'll hear from Charlie or his lawyer by then."

Ryan agreed, and Ashley ended the call. She turned uneasily to the other woman, unsure of whether Patty would be her usual, friendly self or the cool, distant near-stranger she'd seemed lately. She really wished she knew what was going on with her friend, but now was probably not the best time to explore that path. Besides, between her early morning, the hot sun, and the drama of Charlie's arrest, she was too tired for a long, emotional conversation.

"Hey, girl! How was the fundraiser?" Patty seemed genuinely interested.

"It was murder," Ashley replied, grimacing.

"That bad, huh? What happened—run out of mini eclairs?" Patty laughed.

"No," Ashley said, "I mean it really was murder—on the seventh hole."

"What? What are you talking about? Someone was killed? Who? How? Why?" Patty sputtered in disbelief.

"Yes, Oliver Green, the primary CURE researcher, was bludgeoned on the golf course and left half-buried in leaves. And Charlie Brady has been arrested for the murder. I can't believe you haven't heard at least five versions of the story through the Seagrass grapevine by now."

Patty blushed. "I was—um, I didn't—I haven't seen or talked to anyone yet today." Waving that off, she continued, "Charlie

Brady? Ryan's Uncle Charlie? Uh-uh. No way. There's no way that man would hurt a flea, never mind killing someone. He's a teddy bear! Why on earth does the sheriff think he had anything to do with it?"

"Well, they were golfing partners for the day. Charlie was pretty tipsy before they left for the game, and he was so crocked when he came back inside, I'm not sure he even knew where he was! And I didn't tell the sheriff or Ryan, but he also said something about being ready to kill his partner for being such a nasty winner. It really doesn't look good."

"You're not going to get involved in this one, are you? I know you've helped the police in the past, but it's so dangerous. This isn't a creep stealing from a distance, through a computer; this person didn't mind killing someone 'up close and personal,' as they say, and I bet he or she wouldn't hesitate to kill again if you seemed like a threat to his or her freedom. Please tell me you're going to stay out of it this time!"

"No, no; I'm going to let the police handle this one," Ashley assured her friend. "I told Ryan I'd snoop around when I pick up some things at the clubhouse, but that was really just to help him feel better. This time, it's all on the sheriff's department to figure it out. I'm too busy for detective work right now, anyway," she added, not quite believing her own words.

Patty nodded, clearly relieved.

"On the bright side," Ashley added, "your private dining experience donation brought one of the highest bids in the silent auction. The last bid I saw, just before the auction closed, it was up to $1300. That should be great advertising for the business!"

"I know—the auction chair already contacted me to tell me that the winner is hoping I'm available this weekend, on Sunday evening. It's his thirtieth wedding anniversary, and he'd like to make the catered dinner part of his gift to his wife. Can you imagine spending that much for *a part* of a gift? Anyway, that's really, really short notice—just three days—and I don't think I can pull it off on my own that soon. Could you help me? Between the two of us, I think we can make it work."

"Sure, I'd love to help! How about we get together tomorrow afternoon to make plans?" This might be the perfect chance to try to re-connect with her friend and figure out why they had been drifting apart. She worried that Patty didn't approve of her sleuthing, that maybe she felt like Ashley wasn't taking her catering business seriously enough and leaving her partner to handle more than her fair share of the work. "My event tomorrow doesn't start until four, and I can finish up the last-minute prep while we talk."

"That would be great! I have to meet someone now, but I'll see you about one o'clock to-morrow, if that's okay. In the meantime, if there's anything I can do to help you or Ryan with this mystery, let me know. You aren't fooling me in the least; I know you too well to believe you're going to step back and leave it to the police." Patty gathered her things and waved good-bye as she scooted through the kitchen's back door.

CHAPTER 5

The sun was peeking around the edges of the frilly eyelet curtains when Ashley woke up the next morning. She was about to check the clock to see if she had time for a little more sleep when something wet and cold hit her exposed back where her shortie PJs had a little gap.

"DIZZY!" she shrieked. Her dog gave her a “Who, me?” look." Dizzy, if I didn't know better, I'd swear you did that on purpose so you could laugh at me! You just took 5 years off my life, you silly mutt!"

Dizzy cocked her head to one side as if she

was considering what Ashley said. She barked and then, taking the hem of Ashley's tee in her teeth, she tugged to tell her mistress that time was wasting and that Ashley needed to get moving.

"You are a tyrant, Miss Dizzy! Okay, okay—I'm getting up. What time is it, anyway?" Ashley groused as she headed to the kitchen to start the coffee and let the dog outside. "Ugh! It's only 6:30, Dizzy; I don't have to be anywhere until nine, but you couldn't let me have one single day to sleep in, could you?" The feisty rescue dog, a lab-hound dog mix, didn't react to her mistress' voice as she trotted through the bedroom door and toward the kitchen, toenails clicking on the hallway's wood floors. She was clearly on a mission to find breakfast, and she wasn't going to be distracted from it.

Following the dog into the light-filled kitchen, Ashley measured rich, dark-roast coffee and filtered water into the coffeemaker on the counter, then filled Dizzy's bowl with kibble before grabbing her phone. "*Up early, thanks to Dizzy. Meet at diner in a half hour?*" she texted Ryan, figuring they might as well get an earlier start to their day.

She made it all the way into the bathroom and had turned on the shower before she heard the ding of Ryan's reply. "*Your dog is a menace! But yeah, I'm awake now so c u there.*" She could just imagine Ryan's tousled bedhead as he pecked at the keys with one eye still closed.

Not sure of what her day held in terms of any investigation, she slid into a sundress that was polished enough for professional meetings but cool enough for the hot summer day, knowing that her afternoon client wouldn't mind that she wasn't wearing her standard chef's uniform, and stuffed a pair of shorts, a tee, and her kitchen clogs into a beach bag. She could change into the work clothes when she finally got to the kitchen and then back into the dress and some pretty summer sandals for the afternoon's tea event.

"Dizzy Doll, I'm leaving. Your water and food dishes are full, so stay out of the garbage can today, and stay off the furniture!" Ashley was sure that Dizzy was doing thc doggy equivalent of rolling her eyes, and that she would be comfortably ensconced on the bed before Ashley got out of the driveway.

As she walked to the car, she noticed her neighbor, Elena Montez, who was picking up her newspaper. The elderly woman waved and called out, "Good morning, Ashley! You're out early!"

"Yes, ma'am; I'm meeting Ryan for breakfast at the diner." She caught herself before she said anything more. Mrs. Montez was a sweetheart, but she did have a tendency to gossip if she got hold of a hot tidbit.

"Oh, that sounds good! Give him a hug for me, won't you?" She turned to go back indoors, then stopped, apparently remembering something. "I almost forgot! Dear, I noticed that the begonias on your porch need a bit of deadheading. Would you mind if I clip them back for you and get a few cuttings at the same time? Your flowers have such unusual colors, and I would love to root some for my great-niece; she loves flowers, and she could use a little cheering up these days."

Ashley knew that the niece had been ill for several weeks following a bout of appendicitis. "Of course; help yourself, and tell Malena hello for me. I hope she's feeling better!" Glancing at her watch, she exclaimed, "Uh-oh! I'm going to be late. I'll talk to you later, Mrs. Montez. Have a great day!" She hurried down the drive to her fire-engine red VW Beetle hatchback and headed out toward the town's main drag.

When she got to the restaurant, Ashley sat in her car for a minute to appreciate the old-style sign over the door, with its stylized coffee cup and simple font, and the crisp gingham curtains in the windows. The Seagrass Diner had opened in 1923, and the same family owners had fed the generations of the town without a break ever since. It was homey and comfortable, even if it was a bit old-fashioned. The menu was filled with old-style comfort foods, and her mouth was practically watering as she thought about the diner's renowned hot, fresh-made biscuits.

She stepped inside and looked around for Ryan. Nearly all of the red leatherette-covered booths and counter stools were full, but she finally spotted Ryan near the kitchen doors. He looked tired, but he smiled when he saw her come into the diner and waved her over.

"Good morning, Ms. Ashley! And how are you this beautiful morning?" She turned to find an older man smiling at her.

"Good morning, Mr. Kelsom, I'm just fine, thank you. How is the hardware business going?" Smiling back, she signaled Ryan that she'd just be a minute.

"Oh, as long as I attend to the nuts and

bolts of the business, we do just fine," he replied, eyes twinkling. The hardware store owner was well-known and loved for his puns and his dry wit. She enjoyed talking with him; he always made her laugh, no matter how her day might be going.

Playing along, Ashley groaned before giving him a quick hug, then headed back to the booth where Ryan sat, looking decidedly less cheerful than the hardware store owner.

"Coffee, please, Mags," she told the waitress. "And I'll figure out breakfast by the time you get back!"

"You mean you'll figure out that you want biscuits and gravy, with a side of bacon and grits, like you do every time you come in for breakfast," the waitress teased. "We both know you aren't going to order the oatmeal and fruit that you always say you should eat!"

Laughing, Ashley handed over the menu. "Okay, Maggie, you've got me. Bring me the usual! I hate to be so predictable, but not enough to miss out on those biscuits. Just for fun, how about a glass of orange juice this morning, too?"

After the waitress walked away, Ashley asked, "What's up? Have you talked to Charlie this morning? Have the detectives told you anything more?"

Ryan shook his head without looking up. "No. I haven't talked to him yet, and the deputies aren't talking to me. They couldn't question him about the murder because he was drunk; apparently someone who is drunk or drugged up can't legally waive his Miranda rights. They just charged him with public intoxication so they could hold him overnight. I think part of the reason Mueller let them charge him was so they could keep an eye on him, just in case he needed to go back to the hospital. The last I heard was that he would be arraigned sometime this afternoon. But this morning enough time should have passed for him to sober up enough that they can interrogate him. They'll probably charge him for the murder before the hearing."

"I just can't believe they would charge him on such flimsy evidence. I'm sure he'll be bonded out today. There's no reason the judge shouldn't set bail at the hearing. Charlie's a life-long resident with family and a business in the community. And he's got the money for the bond; you'll have him home tonight, I'm sure."

"Maybe," Ryan grumped, "but I'm not so sure he should be home. I know he didn't murder anyone, but he was so drunk. He's a danger to himself; at least in jail, he can't get to the booze! And, the way things are going, he's going to be railroaded straight into prison for someone else's crime."

"C'mon, Ryan, don't give up yet. Sheriff Mueller won't let them send Charlie away without evidence, and we know there's no evidence because Charlie didn't do it. And we're going to find out as much as we can to help figure this thing out. You've got to hold on; I can't do this one by myself."

"Yeah, I know. Mueller's fair, but he's convinced that Charlie killed Green, and I'm not sure the department is even looking for anyone else; they think they have a slam-dunk case all wrapped up. I'm going to try to talk to the detective in charge of the investigation later, but I doubt it will do any good. Where do we even start on this?"

"Were you able to get anything from the GPS check?"

"Not yet; I worked for a while last night, but I fell asleep before I got the info." He looked a little sheepish.

"Well, that's not surprising; you had a long, stressful day, so, of course, you were exhausted. Besides, you'll be more useful after a little rest, and those few hours won't set us back that far. What's on your schedule for today? How much time can you spare from business?"

"I don't have any client meetings today, so my time's pretty much my own. What should I do first?" He started to look a little more hopeful as they continued to talk.

"Why don't you keep working on the GPS thing? I think I'll head to Victoria to check out Green's lab at the U of H campus. I should be able to talk to someone at the lab, do a little snooping at the clubhouse and still be back to the shop in time for the tea party. Everything is baked and prepped; I just have to set things on the trays, set the tables and make the tea, so I'm fine as long as I get to the kitchen by three. I'll call Patty and tell her I'll meet with her after the tea."

They finished breakfast, paid the bill and headed out, agreeing to talk again that evening.

"Oh, Ryan," Ashley stopped him as another idea hit her. "If you have time, see what you can dig up about Oliver Green. The books and mystery shows always start by getting to know the victim. Maybe there's something in his past to explain what happened."

He nodded. "Couldn't hurt."

They waved good-bye and headed off to complete their tasks.

CHAPTER 6

Ashley considered how to get someone at the lab to talk to her and what she wanted to ask as she made the short drive to Victoria. When she could only think of the classics from her favorite mystery stories, like "Did Dr. Green have any enemies," and "Who might want to hurt him," she decided to just go with the flow, to improvise as things unfolded. She hoped that there would be an opening in the conversation that would lead her to what to pursue next. She found a parking spot in a visitors' lot and walked to the science building. Inside, she stopped a couple of backpack carrying students who were vigorously discussing a soccer game they'd watched the night before, accompanied by a lot of head-shaking and wide, emphatic arm and hand gestures.

"Excuse me—can you tell me where Dr. Oliver Green's lab is located? He's the head of the CURE project, I think." She hoped they wouldn't ask why she wanted to know, given the death of the researcher.

"Sure, it's on the second floor—the whole floor. But I don't think anyone is up there today; Dr. Green died yesterday, so I think they closed down the lab for a few days." The student pointed to a staircase at the end of the hall, not showing any curiosity about who she was or why she was asking.

"Thank you. I guess I'll take a chance that someone might be there." Ashley hurried away before the two young people could realize that her presence was a little odd and decide to ask any questions, but she had nothing to worry about. They had already gone back to arguing about the officials for the game and weren't paying any attention to her at all.

When she stepped off the staircase, she was facing a double door with a small white plaque on the wall, labeling the room simply "Lab." She stepped inside with the plate of beignets she'd brought to express her condolences. After all, people always seemed more talkative when presented with a plate of desserts, and that was exactly what she needed. There was only one person in the lab, and Ashley began to relax. It couldn't be too hard to convince just one person to talk, could it?

"May I help you?" The young man walked over to the short wall dividing the lab from the entrance. "I'm afraid I'm the only one here. We've had a death on the team, so the lab is closed today." He eyed the French doughnuts hungrily, so Ashley offered him the plate. He set it on the counter, stuffing one beignet into his mouth while grabbing another to hold in reserve.

"Hello, my name is Ashley, and I'm working with the sheriff's department, investigating Dr. Oliver Green's death. I wonder if you could answer a few questions for me?" She crossed her fingers, hoping he wouldn't ask for any kind of official identification.

" I guess. I'm not sure how helpful I can be; I was in Corpus yesterday, surfing, so I don't know anything about what happened except what the others told me last night. Oh, and I'm Blake." He brushed the powdered sugar off his hand and stuck it out to shake hers.

"Thanks, Blake. I'm hoping you can help me understand a bit more about Dr. Green and his colleagues. How well did you know him?"

"I'm an intern on the project; he was my boss. He was in charge of the lab, so we all worked for him, really. Of course, lowly interns don't spend much face time with the boss, but there are only six or seven of us working here most of the time, so we do get to know each other pretty well, at least professionally."

"What did you think of him? Was he good at his job?" Ashley hoped she wasn't asking too much too soon. She didn't want him to feel like she was interrogating him; keeping it casual would be much more likely to get her the information she needed.

"He was brilliant. The research going on here is ground-breaking, and it was his baby. We are about to wind up the clinical trials and, if the data holds up to analysis, there could be a cure for cancer on the market in a matter of months. Based on the preliminary data, the FDA has already accepted our application for approval consideration." Blake was clearly proud to be a part of the success of the research.

"What's it like to work in the lab?" Ashley wasn't sure what she was looking for, so she was relieved when Blake seemed to understand the question better than she did herself.

"Trials are stressful for everyone. There's a lot of work—someone works pretty much around the clock, every day—and there's a lot riding on the work. If we do this right, millions of lives could be saved, so there's always that shadow over you, making you really conscious of not wanting to make any kind of mistakes. It can make people snap at each other, but most of us get along pretty well."

"If the trials are drawing to an end, what's next? Was there still going to be work going on? Or was this a chance to relax and rest a bit?"

"Oh, sure. The data still has to be analyzed and then the academic paper has to be written and published. And, of course, the FDA—the Federal Drug Administration, that is—still has to approve the drug for the market. It will still take a few months, but that's not so long when it means being recognized as the man who cured cancer!"

"That makes sense," Ashley acknowledged. "You said you were away from the lab yesterday?"

"Well, most of the day. I was in for a little while in the morning, but I left around noon to go surfing. One of the other staffers was supposed to be in around one o'clock, so I headed out to the beach. Even Green would have understood taking a lunch break, so I didn't think he'd mind that I closed things up for an hour."

Ashley mentally crossed her fingers and asked, "Do you know of anyone who might want Dr. Green dead? Did he have any enemies?"

For the first time, Blake looked a little hesitant about talking to her. "Well, most people really didn't like him very much. He—well, he wasn't very popular."

"Oh? Why was that?"

Blake grimaced. "Well, he was pretty rude to nearly everyone. It got so bad with the families of the trial participants—you know, those trying the new drugs—that he was pulled from actual patient interaction; he treated them really badly. And he was just so intense; he expected everyone to be at the top of their form all the time, with no let down. He could be pretty tough if he thought someone was slacking off."

He took a deep breath. "Plus he was constantly harassing the women in the lab, especially Dr. Graham—Wendy Graham; she's co-PI, you know, the Principal Investigator who is leading up the grant-funded research project. He was always hitting on her, even when she rejected him, which she did every time. He would proposition her more than once just about every day, and he had his hands all over the other female lab staff. And, of course, there was a lot of professional competition; after all, in order for Dr. Green to win the prize for being the first to develop a cure for cancer, someone else has to lose. I don't think anyone would kill him for any of those reasons, though; I mean, that's a pretty intense reaction!"

Nodding, Ashley started to ask another question, but they were interrupted when another young man walked in, giving her an inquiring look.

She reintroduced herself. "Hello, my name is Ashley Adams. I'm so sorry for your loss. Could we talk for a few minutes about Dr. Oliver Green? I'm helping the police with their investigation." She felt a little guilty about the half-truth, but she *was* helping them; they just didn't know about it and they weren't aware they needed any help in the first place. She was only stretching it a little, not really lying outright.

"Thank you," the man muttered, looking past her as he accepted a beignet from the plate she proffered. "I'm Evan Richard. I wish I could help, but this is a critical time in our work, and we don't have time for trivial distractions. I'm a PhD candidate working with Dr. Green and Dr. Graham and with Dr. Green—umm, gone, I have a lot of work to do to make sure it moves forward."

"How well did you know Dr. Green?" Ashley watched as a dusting of powdered sugar from the beignet danced on Evan's upper lip when he spoke, thinking it a little weird that he considered the murder of his boss nothing more than a distraction.

"Well, he was my employer and mentor. I've been working with him since the project's beginning. I knew him about as well as anyone, I guess. We were pretty tight." Evan finally wiped his mouth with the back of his hand. "You know, I really want to honor his legacy by keeping the trials and the publication on track. It's the least I can do for him; he was my mentor, and I owe him a lot. So, I'm sorry, but I really need to get to work; I simply don't have time to talk about anything that isn't related to the project. Please excuse me." He grabbed another beignet off of Ashley's tray and headed to the back of the lab with a nod.

Ashley thanked Blake again and left. Remembering Green harassing the young woman volunteer at the tournament, she made a mental note that she definitely needed to talk to Wendy Graham. She also wondered about Evan Richard and his seemingly uncaring reaction to Dr. Green's death. He was certainly an arrogant and confusing young man.

CHAPTER 7

Ashley got back to Seagrass with plenty of time to stop by the country club, pick up the equipment she'd left behind and try to get some information while she was there. She looked around the parking lot, but there were only a few cars parked under some shady trees. Hoping someone could let her into the kitchen, she ventured inside.

"Good morning, Ms. Adams. It's nice to see you back today; is there anything I can do to help you?" Greg was dressed more casually today, and he looked much more comfortable as well.

" I need to pick up some things I accidentally left in the kitchen yesterday. Is there someone who can let me in?"

"I'm not sure, but Stacey, the bartender, is at the bar. She might be able to help you."

Before he could turn back to his post, Ashley plunged in. "How are you after yesterday? I'll bet your evening was crazy, what with the murder and all."

"Oh, yeah, it was intense. I was supposed to get off at six, but I didn't get to leave until after ten. The boss asked me to stick around until the police finished talking to everyone and we could get them on their way home, and we all helped get the food that was supposed to be served at the awards ceremony stashed away. I can't believe someone was killed out there on the golf course, and I would never have thought Mr. Brady would do anything like that!" Greg shook his head and started to walk away again.

"Some of us aren't really sure that he did.

Do you know of any enemies Dr. Green might have had? I mean, I didn't know him, and I can't imagine what would make someone do something like that!" Ashley widened her eyes, trying to avoid looking like she was interrogating the young man.

"Well, he didn't come around a lot, but he wasn't super popular when he did. He was pretty rude, and he was so out of line with the ladies on staff. A real creep." Greg looked around, as if suddenly realizing that he probably shouldn't be talking negatively about members. "Hey, I've got to get back to work. Let me know if you need help with your stuff or anything."

"Hmm. Maybe I need to talk to some more of the women at the lab or here at the club," Ashley thought. "I wonder if some husband or boyfriend could have gotten angry enough to kill him." Ashley shook it off for the moment; she needed to get her equipment and get back to the kitchen. Things for the afternoon tea were under control, but she wanted to be available to help Patty with the planning and prep for the weekend's auction meal.

Stacey was restocking the bar area. "Hi, Stacey! Is the manager here? I really need to get my stuff out of the kitchen this morning."

"Hey, girl! No, Javier's not here, but I have a set of keys now," the bartender replied, holding up a key ring. "I feel really awful about bad-mouthing him yesterday, too. I didn't know his daughter recently passed away from cancer—it's no wonder he's been distracted. I can't even imagine going through something like that. I guess that's a lot more important than whether or not some old coots have more whiskey than they really need."

"Oh, how sad! How did you find out?" Ashley felt bad about prying, but she needed to get all the information she could to help Charlie.

"You know how he went missing yesterday? Apparently, he had some kind of breakdown and had to leave. One of the club's board members convinced him to take some time off to grieve and recover, instead of trying to come back to work so soon. He left right before those two golfers found the dead guy." Stacey looked solemn for a minute. "I'm just glad they didn't make me the interim manager; that's a headache I can definitely do without. Handling members in the bar is plenty for me, and I'd hate spending so much time shut away in an office instead of talking to folks."

Ashley nodded farewell and collected her equipment from the kitchen. As she walked back to the car, her phone began to vibrate in her pocket.

"Mayday! SOS! And all those other emergency things! We have a crisis—can you come to the kitchens right away?" Clearly, Patty was in a panic.

"On my way—be there in 10" Ashley texted back, wondering what was going on. "*RU OK?*"

"*No injuries—just hurry PLEASE!!!*" came

back almost instantly.

She walked into the back door of the kitchen to the banging and clanging of pots and Patty's French-laced swearing. "What's going on? What's got you in such a frenzy?" Ashley asked, ducking as a dishtowel came flying towards her.

"Augh! Tonight—it's tonight!" Patty wailed. "They want the auction dinner tonight instead of Sunday! How am I supposed to prepare a five-course meal with less than eight hours' notice?"

"That's not good, but we can pull this together, so calm down. What's in the freezer that we can work with?"

"I promised them coq au vin as the main entrée, but I have to prepare an appetizer, a soup-and-salad course, some kind of fish and dessert. I've been getting everything ready to go into the oven for the chicken; I haven't even had a chance to look for the rest."

"Okay, I'll see what's in there. I think you

put some butternut squash bisque in there, and I know I've got some pastries. There's not enough time to make the tarte tatin like I'd hoped, but I have extra chocolates I won't need for this afternoon, along with some profiteroles that we can fill with cream and jam. How about a shrimp crepe for the seafood course? And we can do a simple salad with romaine lettuce, dried cranberries, and toasted walnuts. There should be some of your raspberry vinaigrette left, too; it's perfect with the salad, especially with a bit of blue cheese crumbled on top."

Patty took a shuddering breath. "That's not super fancy, but I think it's perfect on such short notice. We have some grainy rye bread that would make the perfect croutons to float on the soup, and I picked up some lovely asparagus this morning. It would pair beautifully with shrimp and Mornay sauce to fill the crepes without making that course too heavy. And I'm pretty sure there's some lemon sorbet that would go well with the pastries; we could use that lemon curd you made last week to fill them instead of jam, and then we can drizzle it all with a raspberry sauce. You, girl, are a genius!" She grabbed Ashley and wrapped her in a bear hug.

They spent the afternoon pulling together their improvised menu. Ashley slipped out to serve the ladies attending the afternoon tea in the front dining area, promising to meet Patty at the auction winner's home by 6:00 to set up the romantic meal for two.

"Patty, this meal is spectacular," Nancy commented. "It was the perfect meal for our thirtieth wedding anniversary." Nancy reached for the hands of her husband Robert, a CURE board member, across their own dining room table. They had clearly enjoyed the dishes Patty and Ashley labored over at the last minute and had held hands most of the evening. It was easy to see why their marriage had lasted for so long.

"Wait until you taste the dessert," Patty said, smiling. "You'll definitely feel like there's a party going on when you get a bite of Ashley's profiteroles and lemon curd. And the chocolates are divine!"

As the couple enjoyed their dessert, the two friends began clearing things away in the kitchen. They could hear Robert and Nancy talking and, when the conversation turned to the murder, the chefs stopped to eavesdrop openly, huddling close to the swinging service door between the kitchen and dining room to catch every word.

“What possible reason would Charlie Brady have for killing Oliver Green? I know Oliver could be a bit arrogant, but, if that's a motive for murder, a lot of local businesses would be missing their CEOs. And Charlie is the kindest, most even-tempered man I know. I refuse to believe that he's hurt anyone, even for a better reason than a nasty argument over a golf game."

"Well, some of the board has just been informed that someone was embezzling funds from CURE; Joe discovered it when he went in to deposit the tournament proceeds and realized that the balance didn't match what it should have been." Robert frowned, thinking about the trouble ahead for the foundation.

"What does that have to do with Oliver or Charlie, though?" Nancy asked.

"No one had access to the account except board members, so it pretty much has to have been an inside job. Oliver was the treasurer, so it would be pretty simple for him to skim now and then. And if Charlie found out and confronted him—"

"But why? He had plenty of money of his own, and he was getting a lot more in grants on top of the CURE money. Why would he need to steal?"

"Rumor has it that Oliver liked to gamble—liked it a lot. I don't know if that's true but gambling debts don't just go away." Robert lifted the last bite of rich chocolate into his mouth and licked the corners of his lips. “I guess it will come out during the investigation of the embezzlement and the murder, if we're lucky. I'm not looking forward to the next few weeks."

Patty looked at Ashley with a raised eyebrow, but said nothing as they washed the dishes from the earlier courses. Back at the kitchen, they discussed what they had learned. "So, Oliver might have been stealing money from CURE," Patty mused.

"If that's true, there must have been a reason. If he really was gambling and losing a lot, maybe he owed someone like a loan shark and didn't pay up fast enough. Maybe that's who killed him." Ashley thought for a few seconds and then continued, "Somehow, that doesn't really feel right. I think I'll try to peek into CURE's financials and Oliver's personal records to see what I can find out."

Patty nodded. "I’m going to assume that by

'peek' you mean something totally legal and above board. Otherwise, I didn't hear anything." She held Ashley's gaze for a few seconds. "While you're at it, you ought to "peek" on the finances for the lab, too, to see if anything's missing there. You know, work *is* everything to some people."

Ashley looked closely at her friend, wondering what she meant by that last statement, if it was some kind of veiled hint. More than ever, she felt sure that Patty didn't approve of her sleuthing, that she thought that Ashley wasn't working hard enough at her baking business, not pulling her weight in their shared business. That had to be the reason that Patty seemed to be pulling away from their friendship, didn't it? What else could it be?

They put away the last of the supplies and said good-night, both ready to finish what had been a long and busy day.

Too tired for anything but her bed, when

Ashley got home, she texted Ryan. *"2 tired 2 talk 2nite; much to tell—CU tmrw."* Snuggling into her pillow, she told her dog, "No early wake-ups, Dizzy girl; we'll have a little lie-in tomorrow, okay? You can have an extra treat for brunch instead of an early breakfast." Without waiting for an answer, she crashed into dreamland.

CHAPTER 8

She had just walked outside with Dizzy the next morning when Ryan pulled into the drive. "Hey, Ryan. "Come walking with us, and we can talk."

The excited dog danced around Ryan's feet as he got out of the car. "Hey, girl! Have you missed me?" Ryan laughed at her antics as she stood on her hind legs and then bounced back down to twirl and hop in a frenetic dance, yelping excitedly until he reached down to scratch her head.

They walked along silently while Dizzy tugged on her leash to explore every tree, bush and blade of grass. along the way. After a few minutes, Ashley raised the subject.

"Ryan, what's going on with Charlie?"

"He's been released, for now. There was no evidence on his clubs or his clothes; his attorney says that there is no way someone hit Green that hard without getting blood spatter on himself. I don't know how long it will last, though. I don't think the detectives are convinced yet that he's not the killer. They keep questioning him again and again, and it doesn't seem like they are even looking for other suspects." He started to say more, but then closed his mouth into a tight line. Ashley was pretty sure of what he had been about to say, but she waited him out, letting the silence build until he broke it.

"Ash, there are so many holes in his story. I know he's innocent, but even I can see the gaps. According to Sean Frazier, one of the deputies, Charlie can't explain why he quit playing early or where he went between then and when he got back to the clubhouse. They think he could have changed clothes before he went back to the clubhouse; no one has been able to remember what he was wearing earlier. Apparently several people at the bar heard him say he wanted to kill Oliver. And you heard what he said to the deputies, that definitely didn't help anything. They don't seem to have any other leads, either." Ryan looked so defeated that Ashley's heart hurt for him.

"I saw him before he went to play; he was wearing the same clothes when he got back. I'll give Sheriff Mueller a call and tell him that."

As they turned back toward the cottage, she asked, "How about the GPS tracking? Have you been able to get a hit on where Charlie was that afternoon?"

"No, I had some problems, and it's taking longer than it should have. I did access Green's emails, though; I thought maybe there would be something there that might help." He looked irritated.

"Was there anything helpful there?" It couldn't have been too incriminating, or he would have already mentioned it.

"Not really; it was all pretty ordinary and boring, except one. Some guy named Jordan Berg sent a threatening note."

"Who's Jordan Berg?"

"According to some social media sites, he's Wendy Graham's fiancé, and he blames their relationship problems on Green. I figured we'd want to talk to him, so I also found out he plays baseball every Saturday morning, about this time—on those new fields about a half-mile from here." Ryan looked pleased with himself.

"Let's go, then! There's no time like the present to find out what he knows." She was surprised by how excited she was about the idea of confronting the man. "Come on, Dizzy, we're going for a ride." The dog's ears perked up, and she started hauling Ashley across the lawn and toward the cars parked in the driveway. "Ride" was one of her favorite words, right behind "treat" and "walk," and she wasn't going to waste any time getting it started.

They got to the field just as the game was ending, and Ryan was able to identify Jordan, who was packing up his equipment, from a picture he'd found online. They introduced themselves and asked if he had a few minutes to talk.

"What's this about? I have to meet my fiancée in a couple of hours, and I need to clean up first, but I guess I can spare a few minutes." Jordan looked puzzled.

"We'd like to ask you some questions about Oliver Green," Ashley replied.

The change in Berg's demeanor was immediate. “I barely knew the guy,” he said, his voice curt. “Wendy worked with him, but we didn't socialize with him. I only met him a few times at CURE dinners and stuff. I don't guess I've talked to him more than five minutes altogether."

He didn't look at either of them, and Ashley felt sure he was hiding something, something they needed to know.

"We've seen the threatening email you sent to him," Ryan stated. "You expressed some pretty strong feelings against someone you say you barely knew. You said you'd make him sorry for what he'd done, and that he'd wish he'd never been born. What did he do to make you so angry?"

"I didn't threaten him; I was just telling him—oh, damn! Okay, I did send that threatening message, but I never intended to do any of what I said there; in fact, I didn't really have anything specific in mind—just 'make you sorry' and that kind of thing. It's just—well, Wendy suddenly postponed our wedding. She said it was because the clinical trials are at such a critical point and the stress of trying to handle that and plan a wedding was too much, but I know it's because of Green. He was too friendly with her; I'm sure they've been having an affair." A vein was popping out on the side of Jordan's head, and his hands were fisted tightly at his sides. He was clearly harboring a lot of resentment and fury.

"What makes you so sure?" Ashley asked. "From all accounts, Dr. Green was giving your fiancée a lot of unwanted attention. No one has suggested she did more than tolerate it — in fact, they say she rejected every advance he made. Maybe she was just trying to get along with her colleague long enough to finish their project on time."

He shook his head. "No. There was more to it than that. I found—" He sighed deeply and covered his eyes. "I spied on her; I started tracking her using a Find My Phone app and she was spending so many late nights at the lab. I figured out her security PIN and, one day while she was in the shower, I took her phone and read her texts." He pulled out his phone to show them a screen shot of the texts.

“I’m not proud of what I did, but check out what I found.”

Wendy: We can't just act on our feelings so quickly.

Oliver: We have to. I can't live like this, with these lies.

Wendy: I need some time to think about it. All that we've built together is at stake.

Oliver: I will give you until Wednesday afternoon. After that, I'm taking things into my own hands and telling them everything.

Berg shuddered, tears filling his eyes. "What else could it mean except that they were having an affair, and he wanted her to break it off with me?"

It certainly looked that way. Maybe Blake in the lab had misread the signals between Green and Wendy Berg; maybe they were having an affair and trying to find the courage to tell her fiancé and their colleagues. Still, there was something about the wording that bothered Ashley, if she could just figure out what.

Ryan asked, "Where were you during the time when Dr. Green was killed?"

"I was supposed to be picking up Wendy at the club so we could go out for an early dinner, but I was about 30 minutes late. I stopped to pick up some flowers for her, and it took longer than I expected."

Ashley wished it shocked her more to discover that a seemingly nice guy like Berg would spy on his fiancée, but she had seen so much worse. Heck, she had done so much worse. She brushed aside those thoughts and thanked him for his time.

CHAPTER 9

Ryan texted her that evening. *"How about a road trip? Let's go to Corpus—aquarium, then horseback ride on beach?"*

"Sounds great! Come for lunch here first about 11."

Dizzy must have been tired, because she didn't wake Ashley the next morning until after eight. Ashley looked up at the soft woof and smiled. Stretching, she looked around the comfortable room, with its antique iron bedstead, topped by a quilt handmade by her great-grandmother. She loved the log cabin pattern made from worn clothes and other household fabrics; it was fun to find scraps she recognized and pull up the memories associated with them.

A louder bark brought Ashley out of the bed, and they went into the warm farm kitchen. She loved her cozy cottage, but she adored the kitchen, with its painted concrete countertops, farm-style sink and bright yellow glass-fronted cabinets filled with bright Fiestaware plates and bowls. She'd found a vintage stove and refrigerator that gave the homey room a 1940s look and rounded out the décor with an old-style dinette set, complete with metal strip around the edge of the table and Formica tabletop. The wide bay window sported ruffled calico curtains, and the walls and countertops showed off her collection of hen and rooster prints and figurines. The only anomaly was her top-of-the-line coffee maker on the counter, looking something like the dashboard of a spaceship.

While the coffee brewed, Ashley slipped into the bathroom, smiling as usual at the painted clawfoot bathtub. She and Patty once spent a silly evening of wine, pastries, and paint creating the whimsical garden on its side, complete with wildflowers, garden gnomes, and little animals and lizards peeking from behind leaves and fronds. After a quick shower, she dressed for the trip in worn jeans, a black tank top, and rich mahogany-colored boots, taking a long-sleeved silver button-down shirt and a San Antonio Spurs cap for sun protection, before getting her first cup of coffee.

"C'mon, Dizzy—let's go outside," she called. The dog raced to the French doors at the back of the open living area, nearly colliding with them in her eagerness to get to the backyard. Laughing, Ashley let them both out onto the wide veranda covering the whole length of the cottage and settled into her rocking chair to look out over her beautifully landscaped yard. By the rear picket fence separating her place from the beach, ruby-red tomatoes, bright green bell peppers, and deep purple Japanese eggplant filled raised beds. Eggplant Parmesan and a fresh salad for lunch, she thought. Scattered around the rest of the space, colorful wave petunias, zinnias, daylilies, and begonias spilled from galvanized watering troughs and wash tubs, while potted hibiscus plants and plumeria trees finished out the tropical feeling.

Finally, she gathered herself and headed inside. After quickly sweeping and mopping the living area's floors and running a dust cloth over the bookshelves and shabby chic furnishings, she went into the kitchen to prepare lunch. As she sliced the eggplant, grated mozzarella and Parmesan cheese, and diced tomatoes, bell peppers, cucumbers, and red onions, she started to consider the murder case, but her thoughts soon turned to Ryan and their relationship. They'd shared a cubicle at SmithCorp after college, where they quickly began commiserating over their dead-end IT jobs. Although Ryan was involved with his college girlfriend, they were several hours apart, so he and Ashley spent a lot of time exploring new restaurants, catching the latest movies, and doing other "date" types of things without pursuing any deeper relationship. Ryan eventually called it quits with his girlfriend, but Ashley had already fallen for Serge and his charms. She still saw Ryan at work and occasionally went to lunch with him, but it seemed any romance between them was unlikely.

As she dredged the sliced eggplant in breadcrumbs and put it under the broiler, she thought about her last birthday at SmithCorp. Stirring the marinara sauce simmering on the back burner, she looked at her sweet pet and sighed.

"Oh, Diz, I made so many mistakes. I remember that day, though; Ryan and I got back to the office, and the first thing I saw was that vase of gorgeous pink roses on my desk. I didn't know who had sent them, but I had the strangest feeling as I watched Ryan's face." The dog cocked her head to the side, as if listening, and then she stood up on her hind legs to offer her mistress comforting doggy kisses.

Ashley smiled at her dog before she continued to think aloud. "My chest felt like a balloon, inflating more and more with each breath. I think I wanted those flowers to be from Ryan even then, but I couldn't admit it. It felt like that balloon popped inside of me when I looked at the card and saw Serge's signature. I hadn't seen or heard from him in several weeks, and his mysterious charisma was wearing off. For the rest of that day, I wanted to bite someone's head off for the rest of the day. Then I made the worst mistakes of all, and I never found out how Ryan felt."

She pulled the tender eggplant out of the oven and topped it with the fresh marinara, some mozzarella and Parmesan, then popped it back into the oven to melt the cheese. As she layered tomato slices, basil leaves, and fresh mozzarella slices, drizzling them with balsamic vinegar, the doorbell rang, cutting off her reminiscing.

"Hey, Ryan. Lunch will be ready in just a couple of minutes; I only need to heat the bread, and we can eat. How about a glass of tea while you wait?"

"That sounds great. It's pretty warm out there, but it's supposed to cool down some this evening, so it should be comfortable riding on the beach. Hi, Dizzy—how's my girl?" Ryan reached down to scratch between the excited pup's ears.

They rehashed what they had learned while they ate.

"I talked to Adam Luna," Ryan reported. "He's the detective in charge of the case. He said Uncle Charlie was feeling pretty rough, but he's coherent again. They're still holding him, waiting for the test results on the golf clubs and clothes. He did tell me that, based on the autopsy, he doesn't think a club was the murder weapon; he thinks Green was hit with something heavier. I'm still not sure if he's looking for other suspects, but I think he may be open to hearing if we find anything that does point elsewhere."

"Well, that's a start. I found out yesterday that Green wasn't very popular at the lab or at the club. He was arrogant and rude, and he hit on just about every female he met. I also found out that Javier Ortiz, the club manager, was missing about the time of the murder—apparently he had a melt-down and was sent home for a few days of bereavement leave. And night before last, Patty and I overheard a conversation about the possibility that Green had a gambling problem and might have stolen money from the CURE accounts. We don't have any definite suspects yet, but we do have a few more leads. Maybe we should have another talk with the detective?"

Ryan agreed and called while Ashley put their dishes into the dishwasher. "Luna's at the station and says he could spare a few minutes to talk with us."

"Let's go, then. I've got some cookies left from yesterday's tea party; we'll take those to smooth the way."

Detective Luna met them in the station lobby. After greeting them, he invited them into a small conference room near the public area. "We'll be more comfortable here. My office is about the size of a small closet, and my partner is interviewing a witness to another case in there, anyway. So what can I do for you today?"

Ryan signaled for Ashley to start things off, so she took a deep breath. "We've learned some things related to the Oliver Green murder that we think you should know and might not have heard yet." She paused, nervous about the detective's reaction; so far, his face hadn't changed, giving them no clue to what he was thinking.

"I found out that Dr. Green was pretty unpopular; the staff at the golf club said that he was rude to most of them and that he sexually harassed the female staff members. The intern at the lab said that Green was obnoxious there, too, and that the women in the lab were tired of his constant come-ons. Then, the night before last, my partner and I were catering dinner for one of the CURE board members, and we overheard him saying that someone had been embezzling CURE's money. He said that Oliver Green was rumored to have a gambling problem and that, as the group's treasurer, he would have easy access to the funds. Maybe some husband or boyfriend lost it when Dr. Green hit on his fiancée or girlfriend, or maybe he owed someone dangerous a lot of money and couldn't pay it back. The point is, a lot of people other than Charles Brady had plenty of motive for wanting the man dead."

"Is that it?" the detective asked. His body language still gave nothing away, but Ashley was encouraged that he hadn't thrown them out yet.

Ryan picked up the story. "Actually, it's not. We talked to Jordan Berg, too. He's Wendy Graham's fiancé; she worked with Dr. Green as co-Prinicipal Investigator on the cancer drug project. Berg was angry with Dr. Green, whom he blames for problems with his engagement, including a postponement of the wedding. He sent a pretty nasty email to Green after reading a text exchange between his fiancée and Green that seems to indicate they were having an affair and that he wanted to tell Berg about it."

The detective sat for a moment without speaking, then he replied, "Ms. Adams, Mr. Bregar, I understand your concern about Mr. Brady; I really do, and I appreciate you sharing what you've learned with me. But there's no evidence in what you've discovered, nothing that proves anyone else had the opportunity or the means to kill Dr. Green. So far, everything we've found points to Mr. Brady." He held up his hand as Ashley and Ryan both began to object. "Hold on—I'm not dismissing what you've discovered. I will look into it, but the reality is that it isn't enough to get your uncle off the top of the suspect list. And, if you're right and our murderer *is* someone else, that person isn't going to be too happy about your poking around and asking questions. I've talked to the sheriff, and he told me about how Ms. Adams' persistence has helped in the past, so I'm pretty sure telling you to stop is a waste of breath and time. But you need to be very careful. Not only could you get yourself into a dangerous situation, you could destroy or put vital evidence at risk. Please, please—if you won't stop your amateur sleuthing, don't do anything stupid—and please keep me in the loop, if you do keep going."

Ashley wanted to feel insulted, but she understood what the detective was saying, and he was a lot politer about it than he might have been. "Detective Luna, we understand your concern, and I appreciate that you listened to what we had to say. I don't know if we'll hear anything else, but we will let you know if we learn something that might be useful. Thank you for your time." They shook hands with the detective and took their leave.

Before starting the car, Ryan looked over at Ashley and said, "Well, that actually went better than I expected. Let's make a deal, though; for the rest of the day, let's forget about Oliver Green, golf tournaments and murder. Let's enjoy the state aquarium, take a slow horseback ride on the beach, and then have a nice dinner at one of the beachfront restaurants. I need a break from all the drama, and I'm betting you do, too."

Ashley agreed. Although she felt like she knew more about the case than she realized, she also recognized that the more she tried to figure it out, the farther the clues would bury themselves into her subconscious. An afternoon without thinking about it sounded perfect.

"I love the Texas State Aquarium," Ashley commented as they pulled into the parking lot. "Every time I come here, I see something I missed the time before." Her eyes sparkled with anticipation. "I feel like a kid, but this is still one of my favorite places."

Ryan agreed. "Have you seen the nursery? Seeing the egg casings and the young jellyfish and octopi is so cool,"

They wandered through the exhibits, relaxing and enjoying one another's company. They visited the underwater viewing room where Shadow and Kai, the dolphins swam and played, and then they walked up to the Islands of Steel display.

"This is interesting," Ryan commented, pointing to a sign "According to this, the oil platforms in the Gulf of Mexico used to be totally dismantled, and that destroyed the habitats that formed around them. Now, they leave part of the platform in place to preserve the new ecosystem with pompano, crevalle jack, red drum, and other fish. I guess it's like what happens around a coral reef."

They continued to explore, touching and feeding the rays in Stingray Lagoon and learning about the tortoises and turtles in Tortuga Cay, then watching the different species of jellyfish, octopi and cuttlefish in the Tentacles exhibit.

Later, as they drove to the equestrian center for their ride, Ashley said, "I think I have a new favorite exhibit now. Eagle Pass looks exactly like a West Texas canyon, and Bonnie, the golden eagle, and Grace, the bald eagle, are so majestic-looking. It's awful that they both have permanent wing injuries that make them non-releasable, but I'm still glad we can see them. Does that make me too awfully selfish?"

Ryan laughed. "No, Ash, I think you're okay there. My favorite was the flower garden with all the parrotfish, blue tang and cownose stingrays. Did you know it's a replica? Maybe we should take the boat out to see the Flower Garden Banks National Marine Sanctuary one day, if there are guided tours around the area."

At the center, they spent a few minutes at the petting zoo, with its common and exotic animals, and then watching the longhorns in their pasture. They debated taking a wagon ride, but decided the beach ride they'd planned would be better. They rode down the public beach at a slow walk, Ashley on a gentle paint named Sadie, and Ryan on Sarge, a beautiful Thoroughbred. They talked easily about the scenery, and Ashley kept them both laughing with stories about her clients and about Dizzy.

After about an hour, they stopped near the dunes to rest the horses and enjoy the sea breezes and the sound of the waves.

"Ash," Ryan hesitated. She looked at him, curious about what he was thinking. "I'm sorry we haven't gone out to dinner yet." She inspected his face for any sign of regret or relief.

"It's okay, Ryan." Ashley responded. "You've been so busy traveling for work and we have seen plenty of each other. I mean we just had breakfast together, so it's almost the same thing."

Ryan furrowed his brow slightly. "Is it?"

"Well, ah, I..." Ashley stumbled on her words, not wanting to say the wrong thing. "No, actually. It's not the same. I was looking forward to..." she hesitated but told herself to be bold. "I was looking forward to a date...a real date with you."

Ryan laughed with relief. "Good! Me too. We'll find a time, soon. I promise, Ash. Once work settles down and Charlie gets out of this mess. I love hanging out with you on days like this, but I want to plan something special. A surprise."

Ashley smiled at him. "That would be great," she said. She felt relieved, because she knew Ryan as a confident guy who was decisive about what he wanted, but since this mess with Charlie, he become very uncertain and tentative. She had been afraid that uncertainty was rubbing off on his feelings towards her.

Ryan picked up a handful of sand and funneled it through his fingers. "You know, I never asked you what happened back at SmithCorp. You don't have to tell me, but I've always wondered why you didn't tell me you were leaving or what happened after that."

Ashley looked down at the sand and drew in a calming breath before speaking. "I wanted to tell you that whole day. I had already resigned, and I knew it was going to be my last day, that I was going to Paris with Serge, but I just couldn't find the right words to tell you. I was just about to say something when Serge surprised me by showing up to pick me up. I was a coward; I chickened out and left without saying anything. Do you hate me for not telling you and avoiding you for the next two years?" She didn't look at Ryan, afraid of what she might see in her friend's face.

"Of course not. I'll admit, I was pretty mad that you just disappeared, and my feelings were hurt. I thought we were pretty good friends, but you just vanished from my life—poof! I didn't know what was going on, but I knew you had a reason for leaving, and I hoped that you'd tell me one day. I was so glad when you came back to Seagrass, even though I couldn't believe you'd left Paris for our simple, unsophisticated little town."

She thought about those days in Paris—the romance, the excitement, the money—and how much she loved it before she found out it was all an illusion. She looked at Ryan and realized that he could be the first person she ever told about it with all the disappointing, embarrassing details.

"I was so sure we were in love, that we would be together forever. Or, at least, I had convinced myself of it pretty well. Serge told me that he wanted us to live in Paris because it would be so romantic; he said we would live near Notre Dame, visit the Louvre, dance at the top of the Eiffel Tower. I dreamed that we'd stroll the Luxembourg Gardens and wander hand-in-hand along the Seine. I had stars in my eyes, and I missed everything else."

Ryan reached over and took her hand, squeezing her fingers but not speaking, giving her time to collect her thoughts and control her emotions.

"Serge told me that we had an assignment from a client that we could complete from Paris. He said that we'd been hired to check the IT security of several brokerage houses; according to him, they had suspicions that someone was trying to hack into their clients' accounts and that we were checking whether anyone had gotten in and to plug any holes in the security. I fell for his story; it seemed so plausible. I hacked into several accounts before he disappeared with another woman, leaving me to answer to the authorities. I found out that he was an international hacker, and all of his money was stolen through fraud, identity thefts, and online scamming. He didn't want to move to Paris for the romance; he wanted to get away from the feds, who were only a couple of days from arresting him. It took weeks for me to convince the French authorities that I didn't know what he was doing; that took Sheriff Mueller vouching for me when they contacted him about my past during their investigation." Ashley's voice was choked with tears that she was determined not to allow to fall. "I was so stupid; I threw away everything to go with him, including our friendship, and he was a fake. I was too dense to see him for what he was—too flattered by his attention to know he was only interested in my computer skills, not in me."

"Ashley Adams, you were not and are not stupid," Ryan retorted. "The rat was a professional; he had years of experience fooling people. Why would you think he was a fraud? You are a beautiful, vibrant woman who would be attractive to any man in his right mind. You had no reason to think he wasn't interested in you!" Ryan paused for a minute. "Look. No matter what happened back then, you're here now, and our friendship is as important to me now as it was back then. I wish you'd felt okay about telling me where you were going, and I wish even more that you'd been comfortable telling me the rest of this before now, but we're still friends. Nothing has changed that, and I don't intend to let go of that. I—" He stopped, seemingly at a loss for words.

"Thank you, Ryan. I haven't told anyone what happened in Paris, at least not all of it. I told Patty that he left me for someone else, and she knows a little bit about the trouble with the law, but not the whole story. I've been so ashamed that I couldn't talk about it."

Ryan wiped away the single tear that slid down her cheek. "Let's go to dinner, Ash. You have nothing to be ashamed of, but, even if you did, it's over and done. Time to forget about that creep and move on. And some fresh seafood and a glass of wine is the perfect place to start. C'mon, woman—get yourself up on that horse, and let's get moving!"

She felt tons lighter. When they were both mounted again, she looked at Ryan impishly and said, "Race you back to the stables—last one back buys dinner!"

Later, as they finished their oysters Rockefeller appetizer and Riesling, Ashley brought up the topic again. "Ryan, there's one more thing. Serge was very angry when the police came around; he was sure that he had me so snowed that I would protect him and tell the authorities that he was innocent. He found out that I told them everything, and he had to take off in the night to avoid arrest. He sent me a letter just before I left Paris. He said that he would never forget what I did to him—yeah, what *I* did to *him*—and that he would have his revenge one day. I don't think he knows I came back to Seagrass, and I haven't heard anything else from or about him since then."

"He'd have to be pretty stupid to come after you; that would just call attention to himself and set the authorities back on his trail. Still, maybe I can do a little discreet digging, find out where he is and what he's up to now." Ashley could already see the wheels whirling in Ryan's mind. "When this thing with Uncle Charlie is straightened out, we'll see what we can discover, if you want." Ashley nodded; their entrees arrived just then, interrupting the discussion. When the waiter left, they turned the conversation to less dramatic topics.

"What's on your schedule this week?" Ryan asked. "Is your catering calendar filling up?"

"We have a couple of events. Tuesday, we're providing refreshments for a mother-daughter teddy bears' picnic tea party. It's going to be cute, I think. The hostess has bought hats and supplies to decorate them, and all the little girls are bringing their teddy bears to share in the party. We're making bear-shaped peanut butter and honey sandwiches, honey candies and lemonade. Patty is making bear pillows—baked pastry rounds filled with ham and cheese—and she had the idea to make bees from rice cereal and marshmallows. Then, on Thursday, we have a pirate-themed party for a scout troop, and we're making pirate cupcakes and treasure map pizza. I usually like the grown-up parties best, but I'm looking forward to these; we're going to have fun with them." Ashley smiled, thinking about the children who would be at the parties.

"What about you? Anything exciting on tap this week?"

He chuckled. "Yeah, sure—designing websites for bed-and-breakfasts and coffee shops is so thrilling. I do have one appointment that could be interesting, though. Do you remember Aleisha Klein and Manny Moreno? I think you went to high school together. They got married about a year ago, and now they're planning to open a doggy daycare business with a tanning salon attached; they also plan to serve brick-oven pizza from that side of the building. I have a feeling that combining all of those into one website could be challenging, to say the least!"

"Dogs, tanning beds and pizza? How on earth did they settle on that combination?" Ashley nearly snorted with laughter. "Come to think of it, though, Aleisha and Manny make a bit of a surprising couple on their own. Manny was quiet in school; he was a terrific athlete, president of the Science Club and voted Most Likely to Succeed, but he never had much to say, and, if he even went to a party, which he didn't much, he'd sit in a corner and watch everyone else. On the other hand, if you looked in the dictionary under 'social butterfly', you'd see Aleisha's picture. She would start up a conversation with a total stranger while standing in the check-out line at the store. It's hard to imagine the two of them ending up together." She shook her head.

"They must have both mellowed since then," Ryan laughed. "We met briefly to talk about their business and to set up another appointment to work out the details of the website. He was definitely in charge, although she joined the conversation with some good ideas. They seem really happy together."

They went on talking about inconsequential topics as they left the restaurant and drove back to Ashley's cottage, where they discussed what they needed to do next on the murder case and then said good-night.

Ashley let Dizzy out into the back yard and curled up in the rocking chair again. "Dizzy, this was a wonderful day. I told Ryan all about

Serge and Paris, and he's not mad at me. I still don't know if he's interested in anything more, but now I know that we still have our friendship. I feel so much better having that much settled. I wonder, though; do you think we could ever be more than friends?"

The dog barked and Ashley laughed. "Of course, Dizzy girl; you're right—we'll just have to wait and see what comes next. Let's go; we have a busy day tomorrow, so it's time for bed."

CHAPTER 10

The next day passed quickly, as Ashley baked cupcakes and made candy for their week's events; Patty took some time off to run errands in Victoria, so Ashley didn't see her during the day. Ryan had stopped by Fresh Start Kitchens to say hello to Ashley and ask what her plans were for dinner.

While Ashley thought about how to answer Ryan, her phone buzzed with a message from Patty. *"Hey, meet at Smoke Daddy Lee's for dinner?"* Ashley thought that maybe Patty wasn't trying to drop their friendship after all.

"Sure—okay to bring Ryan, too?" She knew

Patty would say yes but thought she should ask, after the way things had felt lately.

"4sure—how else 2 talk about case?" Ashley chuckled. "Patty wants to meet at Smoke Daddy Lee's for dinner and a discussion of the case; sound good?"

"Best barbecue in South Texas and you have to ask? How soon do we eat?" Ryan sounded hopeful.

"C U in 20" she texted back to Patty as they left, talking about meaty ribs, smoky brisket, creamy coleslaw and the best cornbread in five counties.

Her parking karma was intact, Ashley found an empty spot right in front of the door to the popular restaurant. The rest of the parking lot was packed, so they knew tables would be at a premium that night, like most nights. Smoke Daddy Lee had the reputation as the king of Texas barbecue, and it wasn't just the tourists who couldn't skip his restaurant on their visits to the area. For locals, the

Smokeground was the closest place to heaven you could get to on Earth; they flocked in to worship the fabulous ribs, sausage and brisket as regularly as they attended church—and even more often for many. While there was a building for indoor dining, many preferred to sit outside. Smoke Daddy Lee had preserved the original setup of his oak tree-shaded riverfront oasis, consisting of a pull-behind smoker latched to a food truck presiding over a herd of wooden picnic tables covered with disposable tablecloths.

"Ashley! Ryan!" roared Smoke Daddy as they walked into the restaurant. "Patty's already here; she said she expected you any minute. Your food will be on the table by the time you finish filling your tea glasses."

Sure enough, when they left the self-serve drink area and found Patty at a table near the back, huge plates of ribs, chicken, and brisket sat beside heaping bowls of potato salad, pinto beans, and coleslaw, alongside heaps of fresh dill pickles, sliced onions, and pickled jalapeños. There were also two baskets—one filled with golden squares of cornbread and the other with crispy jalapeno hush puppies. Squeeze bottles of sauce were labelled "wimpy," "normal" and "blow your head off."

"Oh, man! Smell that smoke! I think I've died, and the angels set the dinner table for me!" Picking up an empty plate, Ryan started to pile it with food.

Ashley and Patty rolled their eyes and giggled. Popping a hush puppy in her mouth, Ashley hummed with pleasure. "This is so good! Hey, Ryan, leave some of that for the rest of us!" She snatched the plate of ribs away from him and looked around for an empty plate for herself.

For a few minutes, the only sounds at the table were slurps and "mmms" of satisfaction. Finally, stuffed, they all leaned back in their chairs. Homemade peach cobbler, Texas chocolate sheet cake, and strawberry shortcake appeared on the table almost like magic, but dessert would have to wait for a little while; they were all too full for even one bite. In the meantime, it was time to catch each other up on the latest in the case.

Patty started off. "What's happening with the murder case? What have you found out? I saw Charlie at the grocery store earlier, so I know he's not in jail anymore. Has the sheriff found other suspects?"

"No, Charlie is still the prime—and only—suspect that the detectives have. We talked to Jordan Berg the other day, though," Ryan said. "He's Wendy Graham's fiancé, and he's dead sure that she was having an affair with Oliver Green. He was mad enough to send a threatening email to Green, but he swears he didn't kill him, that he never really planned to hurt him at all."

"Wow, that's pretty incriminating!" Patty exclaimed. "Do the police know? And do you believe him?"

Ryan looked a little sheepish. "Um, I kind of hacked into the emails, so I didn't think sharing it with the detectives was a great idea. We need to figure out how to let them know about it all, though. But, yeah, I'm not sure why, but I don't think he's our killer."

Ashley took a deep breath before sharing her news. "Ryan's not the only one who's done a little hacking. And what I found isn't good for Charlie. Remember, Patty, how Robert said last night that the board had just found out that someone had been embezzling funds from CURE? Patty? Hey, Patty, are you listening?"

Patty had been looking around the restaurant; she turned back to Ashley. "Oh, uh, sure, I remember. He said he thought Green might have been stealing to pay off his gambling debts because he was the group's treasurer and had easy access to the accounts." Patty still seemed distracted, glancing toward the serving line again. Ashley wondered if it was another sign that Patty disapproved of the time she spent sleuthing, although she did have a shy-looking smile on her face.

"Well, I got into the CURE financials, and it wasn't Green who was taking the money; it was Charlie." She paused, watching Ryan carefully. "Ryan, I'm sorry; I wish I didn't have to tell you."

Ryan shook his head. "It's not your fault, Ash. I kind of suspected that might be what was happening. This really doesn't look good for Uncle Charlie. I think I'll go over there when we finish dinner and try to talk to him again. Maybe—" His voice faded away.

"There's something going on with the lab's accounts, too—thanks, Patty, for suggesting I check those. I'm not sure exactly what all of the financial part means yet, but I did find something else that is pretty interesting. It seems that Javier Ortiz is listed among the trial participants." Ashley hoped that it would turn out to be important enough to balance the news of the embezzlement.

"Who is Javier Ortiz?" Patty asked, still not fully tuned in to the conversation.

"He's the manager of the golf club. The bartender told me that he recently lost his daughter to cancer, and he was at the club the morning of the tournament. Supposedly, he fell apart and was sent home about the time of the murder, but he'd been away from the building earlier, and no one saw where he went when he supposedly left to go home. I think I'll swing by his house tomorrow and see what I can find out. Maybe the breakdown was because he'd just killed Dr. Green."

As Ashley finished speaking, she noticed that Patty was distracted again. Before she could think much about it, Smoke Daddy Lee walked up to their table and greeted them. Patty seemed to forget that Ashley and Ryan were even there as she turned to Smoke Daddy Lee.

"Mmm, yummy! Thanks for a delicious meal again!" Ashley knew Patty was interested in Smoke Daddy Lee, but she was still getting used to watching her flirt. For as long as they'd been friends, Patty was usually all-business.

"Glad you're satisfied, darlin'! I can't have you leaving here unhappy!" Smoke Daddy Lee winked at Patty, who giggled and blushed.

Ryan and Ashley stood up to leave, but Patty didn't seem to hear their good-byes.

CHAPTER 11

As Ashley turned onto Wendy Graham's street, she crossed her fingers in hopes that Jordan Berg wouldn't be at the house. Luck was with her; just as she pulled up in front, a dusty blue sedan squealed out of the driveway, giving her a glimpse of his red, angry face as it sped past her. If they'd been arguing, Wendy might be distracted enough to slip up and give Ashley the clues she needed.

She pulled into the driveway and took a deep breath, calming her nerves and collecting her confidence. As she walked across the lawn to the front door, she noticed that the ground around the brightly blooming hibiscus bushes looked as if it had been disturbed. A little weeding, or had someone tried to hide something in the dirt? Maybe a missing cellphone, even? She'd have to try to find an excuse to check before she left.

"I *said* I'd call when I'm ready to talk to you," Wendy snapped as she opened the door. "Oh, I'm sorry! I thought you were someone else. Is there something I can do for you?" She looked exhausted, and her eyes were puffy and red, like she'd been crying.

"I hope so," Ashley said. "My name is Ashley Adams, and I was the caterer for the CURE fundraiser. I wanted to ask you a couple of questions about what happened that day. May I come in for a minute?"

Wendy looked at the neighboring houses and sighed. "I guess you'd better. I can already see Mrs. Carrolli's curtains twitching. She'll be on the phone gossiping before we close the door."

From what she'd known and heard about Wendy Graham, Ashley expected a modern, practical home, maybe one that was even a bit cold and sterile. Instead, the place had the feel of a seaside home. The furniture was white wicker, while the tab-top curtains and soft pillows added touches of beachy blues, greens and sands. The look was uncluttered, but there were still plenty of photos in shell-lined frames. It should have felt cliché and kitschy, but Wendy had somehow made it all work beautifully. Ashley would love to get some tips from the woman; she loved her own little cozy cottage, but Wendy definitely knew how to make a home feel welcoming.

As they sat, Wendy hugged a seahorse pillow tightly, and Ashley plunged in. "I know Oliver Green was causing you all kinds of problems for a long time. What happened to push you over the edge at the fundraiser?"

"What?" Wendy jumped up from the chair she'd slumped into and threw her hands up, sending the pillow flying. "Are you asking me if I killed Oliver? That's crazy! I would never hurt him that way—or anyone else, for that matter!"

"But he was harassing you at work, to the point that you are postponing your wedding, right?" Ashley watched the other woman's face carefully.

Wendy threw herself back into the chair and covered her face with her hands. After a moment or two, she looked up at Ashley, her expression very close to despair. "Yeah, he was a jerk, and he didn't even realize how obnoxious he was; he thought women were swooning over his attention. To him, the nasty remarks, fondling, and butt-pinches were flirting that I should take as a compliment. He really believed that, when I was shaking from anger, I was trying to hold back my attraction to him!"

Ashley started to respond, but Wendy wasn't finished. "I had it under control, though; I told him Friday morning that I had prepared a formal complaint for the Dean. I told him that I was not interested in his mess and that I never would be and that, if he touched me or made any kind of off-color remark anywhere that I could hear him, I'd make sure that everyone in the university knew what kind of sleazy creep he was."

"What did he say?" Ashley wasn't convinced Wendy had things as much in hand as she said.

"Actually, he ignored me. He had something else on his mind, and, when that happened, he pretty much dismissed everything else." Wendy shook her head, smiling wryly. "As it turned out, what he was worrying over was much more important, and potentially destructive, than sexual harassment."

"Was it your affair he was focused on? Was he breaking it off?" Ashley wasn't expecting the response she got.

Wendy threw her head back and laughed.

"What affair? I would *never* have an affair with Oliver Green! Dear heavens, I couldn't stand to be in the same room with him when we weren't focused on the project; I wouldn't voluntarily spend any extra time with him, much less intimate time. An affair? Ugh. That's just disgusting!"

"Mr. Berg showed us the texts about Green telling someone about your relationship. It sounded like he was pretty adamant about bringing it out into the open and you were just as determined that it stay hidden."

"Oh, for heaven's sake! How did Jordan even see those? Never mind; that's a problem for another time. Apparently, Jordan and I have more to discuss than I thought." She paused, then added, "That wasn't about an affair." A sigh. "Look, that was about our data. The results are really good—too good, in fact. I had this feeling that something was wrong with them, like someone made a big mistake in the math. I asked Oliver about it, and we both went over the data again to double-check the calculations."

"And?"

"And we both came to the same conclusion: either one of the interns screwed up royally or someone manipulated the data on purpose." Wendy looked shaken. "The discrepancies were serious enough that neither of us really believed that it was an intern's math problem. We were pretty sure it was intentional."

"Could it have been Dr. Green who changed it?" Ashley was pretty sure what Wendy would say, but she had to ask.

"No way. The guy was really a creep on a social level, but he was an absolute tyrant about ethics in the lab. He didn't tolerate any hint of dishonesty; he wouldn't even take legitimate shortcuts that might look a little shady. When I told Oliver about my suspicions, he was furious. He wanted to tell the FDA right away; they had already started reviewing our application, and Oliver didn't want them to discover the problem before we reported it. I'm the one who wanted to wait; we've worked for years just to build up to this clinical trial, and I didn't want to throw all of that away on speculation. I wanted to takc a little time to dig into it more, to be sure of what was happening and what it meant in terms of the drug's effectiveness before we told anyone else. Once we were sure, I would have been totally behind him in regards to reporting it; I just wanted to be really certain first."

"Who else in the lab might have done it? For that matter, why would someone do something like that?" Ashley was unsure of the set-up at the lab, who would even be able to falsify the results, much less who might want to do it.

"I've been trying to figure that out myself. It doesn't make sense. The interns wouldn't benefit, and Evan would be the last one who would make that kind of mistake; his grant is about to end, so he's already looking for a spot in another lab. There's no way he'd want to be associated with the fallout from falsified data on a project he'd worked on. I guess some other research competitor could have paid someone to do it, thinking to turn us in later, but I just can't see it; it's totally out of character for everyone I know working in the field, and we all know each other fairly well. I'm still hoping it was just someone's careless calculation error. I'm going over all of the data, all the way back to the rough trial notes and then up to the final reports, to see if I can find out where it started."

"What do you think you'll find? How are the results tabulated and calculated?"

"The interns—there are two—collected the data, then the doctoral students aggregated it for Oliver and me to put into the final paper. The mistake could go back to an intern writing something down incorrectly on the forms they gave to the PhD. students." Ashley fiddled with the engagement ring on her finger and let out a huge sigh. "A careless error by an undergraduate student, and two professional reputations could be ruined. Oliver was always adamant about the fact that interns' names don't go on thc published paper, just his, mine, and the doctoral students'. But they're just starting to make a name, so it's less serious for them. Still, though, it would take that error being repeated many times for it to show up so strongly in the aggregated results. It's just not very likely."

"If it wasn't an error, and someone did manipulate the data, why would they do it?" It didn't make sense to Ashley as an outsider to the whole medical research field.

"That's what we are trying to figure out," Wendy said grimly. "The only reason we came up with would be to make sure the drug was approved, but that was pretty likely to happen, anyway. The real results were still very strong, and it is certain that the drug was highly successful in curing several types of cancer. I can't imagine anyone playing around with people's lives like that—the patients and those of us in the lab—especially when it wouldn't make any real difference to the future of the project. I can't find any way someone would benefit from it."

"Mr. Berg said he was buying flowers for you around the time of the murder. Is that right?" Ashley really wanted it to be true; she felt bad for both of them, and she wanted them to be innocent.

Tears filled Wendy's eyes. "Yes, he picked me up late, and he had that bunch of flowers over there." She pointed to a glorious arrangement of brilliantly colored lilies, roses, and larkspur, along with lush, lime-green foliage. "I can't believe he betrayed my trust by basically cyberstalking me. I think maybe I delayed the wedding because of a gut instinct, but I couldn't admit it to myself, so I blamed it on stress at work. I do love Jordan, but I can't deal with that level of jealousy and insecurity. I can't spend our life together wondering if he's spying on me again."

Ashley saw Wendy steel herself with her words, sitting up a bit straighter as though she were rehearsing a speech she would give later. Ashley could see the heartbreak, which had left the woman drained and worn out. "One last question, Wendy—who are the doctoral students?" That was a question she hadn't thought to ask at the lab.

"Evan Richards and Blake Morrison."

"I thought Blake told me he is an intern?"

"No, he's a PhD. candidate. He's the one who works most closely with the interns, though; he's more or less their supervisor. Evan does most of the data aggregation."

Ashley thanked her and left, feeling bad for adding to the woman's stress and relationship problems and wondering what the things she'd learned meant to the murder investigation.

CHAPTER 12

"Diz, what are we going to do about Patty?" Ashley mused, as she measured flour for a new cookie recipe. "Why is she acting so strange?" Dizzy tilted her head to the right and then to the left, giving the impression that she was carefully considering Ashley's question. She yipped as if to say, “Who knows?” and then plopped down at Ashley's feet.

"Maybe she's right. Maybe I shouldn't be messing around at detecting. I moved back to focus on baking; maybe I should just give up the rest and concentrate on the business." Ashley felt a tug of disappointment at the thought of giving up the puzzles of sleuthing. Or was it something else? "Maybe it's not even the detecting I like. What if I'm kidding myself, and I'm only sleuthing so I can spend more time with Ryan?" She sighed and reached for her canister of sugar just as *La Vie En Rose* rang out from her phone. "And what if I'm wasting that time because he's not interested anymore?"

She grabbed the phone and glanced at the screen. Suddenly flustered, she saw that Ryan was calling, as if thinking about him had summoned him up. After briefly considering ignoring the call, she answered. Maybe he had news about the case.

"¡Hola, mi amigo! What's up?" She winced at how overly perky she sounded. Ryan was sure to think something was wrong, but he didn't seem to notice the fake tone.

"I just wanted to check in with you. I talked to Uncle Charlie last night, and he finally opened up. I just wish what he told me helped clear his name." Ryan's voice cracked with the stress. "Instead, it's more of a mess than ever."

"Why? What did you find out?" Ashley was concerned about the defeat she heard in his voice.

"He confessed to the embezzlement. Ash, it's worse than just overdoing it with the alcohol; he's been using the money to buy drugs. He says it was to help him cope with the divorce; it's really eating him up. He couldn't take that kind of money out of his own accounts without Aunt Mercy and her attorney finding out, so he was stealing from CURE to support his addiction." There was such a long silence on the other end that Ashley thought the call had dropped.

"He checked into rehab late last night, with the sheriff's permission to leave the county. He called me this morning, though, and asked me to visit. Patients usually aren't allowed phone calls or visitors for the first days of treatment, but he says he's starting to remember more about the day of the murder. He wants to talk to me, especially since I told him I had some information about his missing phone." After a few seconds, he continued, "Ashley, I know it's asking a lot, but will you go with me? So much of what he's said doesn't make any sense to me. Maybe, if you hear it, too—well, maybe we can figure it out together."

"Of course I'll go, Ryan; you shouldn't go alone, anyway. When do you want to go? And where exactly are we going?" The thought of being alone with Ryan in the car caused mixed feelings. She liked the idea of spending time with him, but it ruffled her a little, too; she was nervous because she wasn't sure how Ryan felt about her now. Of course, she also wished they had a happier reason for spending time together.

"He's in a place in Galveston. Can you leave now? That would give us time to make the drive, spend some time with him, and still get back before too late tonight."

"Give me twenty minutes to clean up the kitchen and drop Dizzy back at the house. I'll meet you there." Ashley was already covering the dry ingredients she'd measured together and piling the few dishes onto a dishwasher tray as she spoke.

"Okay, see you there. And, Ash? Thank you—really; this means so much to me and to Uncle Charlie."

She assured him that she was happy to help and ended the call. She rushed to finish tidying up and headed home.

"Come on, Dizzy - Ryan needs us. You can make him laugh and I'll help him with Charlie," she told the dog as they climbed into the car.

CHAPTER 13

Ryan was waiting on the front porch swing when Ashley got to the house. "Thanks again, Ash," he said, leaning down to pet the dog. "Hey, why don't we take Dizzy with us? We should have enough time for a quick run on the beach after we talk to my uncle; I bet she'd love it, and it might be relaxing for us, too!" Dizzy put her head on her lowered front legs and looked up at her mistress, whining softly.

"I swear that dog understands exactly what we're saying," Ashley said. "How about it, Diz? Wanna go to the beach and run on the sand?" A bark answered the question, leaving them laughing at the mutt's antics.

"Well, in that case, let me grab a different pair of shoes and an old towel, and we can get going." Ashley detoured through the kitchen to collect some of the cookies she'd baked the night before; Ryan was the perfect guinea pig to test the new recipe on, and it would give them something safe besides the case to discuss.

They drove out along Highway 59, taking the exit at Edna to get to State Highway 35. With only a quick stop in Bay City for some bottled water, they had plenty of time to talk about everything, including their case.

"Have you heard anything about Serge Payton since we talked?" Ryan glanced at Ashley, knowing the topic of her ex-boyfriend was a touchy one.

"No, as far as I can tell, he's still flying under the radar, hoping no one in law enforcement catches a hint of where he's hiding. I think—I hope—that he believes coming after me would give him away." She shuddered to think about the last time she saw her charming and lying ex-boyfriend. "He was furious when I wouldn't cover for him. He thought he'd be kicking back on the beach of a remote island, rich as Midas, by now; he blames me for having to run. He never cared that I almost went to prison because of him."

"You really do attract trouble, don't you?" Ryan teased. "First, it's Payton talking you into hacking into brokerage accounts with his plans to strip them, and now Uncle Charlie and me with murder. Thank goodness Sheriff Mueller believed you when you told him about Payton. Now, if we could convince him that Uncle Charlie's innocent—well, not a killer, anyway."

Ashley brought him up to speed on her conversation with Wendy Graham. They agreed that they needed to find out whether or not Green had told Charlie or the Board about the data problems.

Ashley broached another subject, a little unsure that she really wanted to talk about it. "Have you noticed anything different about Patty lately?" She didn't know if she wanted to tell him what she was thinking, but she was curious what he thought, too.

"Not really; I haven't seen her that much, but that's about it. I figured she was just busy with business. Why?"

Ashley hesitated and then decided to confide in him. "I don't know; it seems like she's been acting kind of weird lately. She seems distant; I keep wondering if she's upset with me—like, maybe she thinks I'm wasting time that I should be spending baking and working with customers instead of sleuthing, both now and back when I was helping the sheriff."

"Hmm. She did seem a little distracted the other night at dinner, but I didn't think much of it. Like I said, I just assumed she'd been busy and was thinking about some event she has coming up. After all, she's the one who brought up the case and started us talking about it. You're best friends, Ash; why don't you just ask her?"

She shrugged, not quite willing to admit that she was a little afraid of what Patty might say and that the conversation might cost her a friend. She changed the subject by handing him a cookie, and they spent the rest of the drive talking about the new recipe and other safe subjects.

On the outskirts of the city of Galveston, Ryan turned into a flower-lined driveway leading to a late-nineteenth century, two-story farmhouse. Its well-kept grounds were inviting, boasting lush lawns and raised beds holding both flowers and what appeared to be vegetable plants. When Ashley commented on the unusual combination, Ryan explained, "Part of the therapy here is working on the edible landscaping. It gets the patients out in the sunshine and working with their hands. And Charlie's doctor explained to me that growing vegetables and then helping prepare them for meals gives the patients a boost of confidence without much risk of failure."

A wide covered porch lined the entire front of the house, with tables, chairs and rockers defining several small areas for conversation. They went inside to find a wide, cool entryway with a reception desk on the left. A staff member came through the door behind the desk as they approached.

"Hi! I'm Maria, one of the nurses. May I help you?"

"Yes, I'm Ryan Bregar, and this is Ashley Adams. We're here to see Charlie Brady. Dr. Ramirez approved it because of the extenuating circumstances."

Maria nodded. "Yes, he told me you would be here, and he explained just enough to be sure I could help as much as possible. Mr. Brady is waiting in the garden for you. I'll show you the way. Would you like some iced tea or coffee while you visit? I can send someone out with it."

Ryan looked at Ashley, and she answered, "That would be lovely. We had a bit of a drive, so something cool to drink would be refreshing." As they passed through a dining room furnished with what appeared to be antiques from the time when the house was built, Maria popped her head into the kitchen.

"Josh, would you mind bringing a pitcher of tea and three glasses out to the garden? Mr. Brady and his guests will be talking out there." Whoever was in the kitchen assured her that he would bring it out right away, and they continued through the doors to the back garden area.

"These stained-glass panels in the door are fantastic," Ashley remarked. "Are they original to the house?"

"No," Maria answered. "One of the first patients here designed and created them. The animals are all symbolic of something important to the healing of our residents, and they are all animals that you might see in Texas. For example, the squirrel represents planning ahead and being prepared, the prairie dog symbolizes community, and the armadillo stands for empathy and personal protection. The birds are special, too; the dove, of course, means peace, the hummingbird is joy, the cardinal is renewed vitality, the eagle shows healing and the owl represents wisdom."

"Wow, I'd never heard about those animals in that context. That makes the panels even more beautiful!" Ashley was impressed by the artwork and by Maria's knowledge of its many meanings.

"Yes, the artist wanted the residents to remember the lessons they learn here whenever they see those animals back home," Maria agreed.

As they stepped onto the small back deck, they took in the casual gardens filled with flowers, trees, and more mixed beds. The smells of rosemary and basil combined with the fragrance of the roses, honeysuckle, and gardenias to create an almost overwhelming perfume. Ashley imagined ladies in long dresses enjoying afternoon tea among the plants, listening to the happy birdsong.

A short bark and a tug on the leash in her hand brought Ashley back to the present as Dizzy spotted Uncle Charlie. She seemed determined to get to him, even though he was a stranger to her. When they were close enough, she looked back at Ashley as if to say, "What are you waiting for? Unhook my leash!" Off-leash, she immediately shoved her head into the man's lap and snuggled in, ducking her nose under his hand to encourage pets. Charlie's shoulders immediately relaxed, although not by much.

"Ryan! Ashley! Thank you so much for coming. And thank you, Maria, for bringing them out to me. I know you're busy, and I appreciate you taking out the time." Charlie smiled weakly at the young nurse, obviously sincere but unhappy.

"Mr. Brady, you know I'll take care of whatever you need! Josh will be out in a minute with some iced tea. You and your friends relax and have your talk. If you need anything, just step into the kitchen and ask Josh to call me." With that, she smiled, waved and headed back inside.

"Charlie, I'm sorry for all the trouble you're having, but I'm so glad you've come here," Ashley tentatively reached out to hug the older man. "Please know we are doing everything we can to get this murder case straightened out, so try not to worry too much about that while you're here."

Charlie looked up at her with tears in his eyes. "I don't know what to say. You are so kind to even talk to me, much less to try to help. I've screwed things up so badly. I don't know if they can be fixed or not, and I'm pretty sure I don't deserve it if they can."

Ashley squeezed his hand lightly to reassure him. Ryan cleared his throat and shifted in his seat before asking, "Uncle Charlie, will you tell Ashley what you told me last night? What you remembered about the golf tournament?"

Nodding, Charlie turned to Ashley. "We started around the course, and Oliver was asking me about my finances. It made me nervous; I was sure he knew I'd been skimming from the donations. I kept drinking from my flask; by the time I realized that he was leading up to asking me to invest in his project, that darned thing was nearly empty."

But the flask was still full when he came into the clubhouse, Ashley remembered. Before she could say so, Ryan asked, "Did Dr. Green say anything specific about the project?" Ashley wondered if he'd told Charlie about the problems with the results.

"He wanted money to help get the new medication on the market. He said he probably wouldn't need the cash right away. In fact, he said that the trial success wasn't even a sure thing and that it could be years away."

"Did he tell you why? I mean, did he explain what he meant about the trials?"

"No, Ryan, and I didn't ask. I thought it was odd, because the board understood that the approval was pretty close, but I didn't want to have to admit that I didn't have the money to invest; I was afraid it would lead to him figuring out I was embezzling from CURE. All I could think was that I needed to finish the round as fast as possible and find another drink."

"You said that your flask was empty, but when I saw you at the bar later, it was so full that the alcohol sloshed out. If you drank all of what you brought and the clubhouse bar was dry due to their inventory issue, how could that happen?" It might not be important, but then again it might turn out later to be significant, so Ashley thought they'd better clear it up now.

"We got to the fifth hole and one of the volunteers, one of Oliver's lab workers, drove up. He stopped to talk to us. It turned out that he also loves good Scotch whiskey, and he had a bottle with him. Between the three of us, we drained it pretty quickly, which is a shame, because it really was good stuff that should have been sipped and appreciated, not guzzled." Charlie gave a weak smirk.

Ryan picked up the questioning again. "Why did you come back to the clubhouse early? Why didn't you stay and finish the game?"

"I've been thinking about that. It's one of the things I couldn't remember, and that didn't make sense to me. Now that I'm sobering up, it came back to me last night; it's one of the reasons I wanted to talk to you about my phone, Ryan. When we were finishing at the sixth hole, I got a call. I don't know who was on the line, but he said that there was an emergency at the clubhouse and that I was needed right away to handle it. Oliver was uncharacteristically generous about it; he told me to go ahead and he'd play through. He said he could use the time to clear his head. That part didn't make much sense then, and I'm still not exactly sure what he meant, but I started back and left him walking toward the seventh hole."

So that was the emergency Charlie mentioned, Ashley thought, not his flask. She didn't mention it, but it did clear things a bit.

"I can't find my phone, so I can't prove there ever was a call. I guess I dropped it somewhere between the sixth hole and the clubhouse. I was hoping, Ryan, that you'd been able to find it." Charlie looked hopeful.

"Well, I did track the GPS coordinates on it, and it got back to the clubhouse but a lot faster than you would have been walking. Maybe someone else found it and brought it to the lost-and-found at the club? You know, someone in a golf cart?"

"If someone turned it in, I haven't heard about it; no one notified me." He hesitated and then shrugged. "That's probably for the best right now, though. I need to focus on rehab and getting sober; a phone would be a big distraction and probably a temptation as well."

Charlie looked like he was tiring fast, and it seemed like he'd shared everything he remembered so far. After exchanging hugs and promises to keep trying to find his phone and to clear his name, Ryan and Ashley wished him well with his treatment and left.

A little later, as Dizzy chased seagulls on an empty section of beach, Ashley and Ryan talked about what to do next.

"I think we need to talk to Javier Ortiz, the club manager," Ashley decided. "His name is on the clinical trial participants list, and his daughter died from cancer recently. Maybe he blamed Green for not saving her. If not, maybe he'll still have something helpful to share. I can go by his house tomorrow before I go to work."

"I'll go back to the club and see if I can track down Charlie's phone," Ryan said. "It won't prove conclusively that he's innocent, but being able to prove he got the call at least will lend credence to his story, and knowing who made the call might be a good lead. In fact, maybe I should talk to Sheriff Mueller and tell him what we've discovered so far."

Ashley agreed. Calling Dizzy back to them, they left the beach to return to Seagrass.

CHAPTER 14

The house number painted on the mailbox confirmed the address she'd found for Javier Ortiz. Ashley pulled to a stop in front of the house and sat for a minute, taking in her surroundings while thinking how to approach her conversation with a grieving father.

An older cottage-style home, the house itself looked to be in good repair and had been painted within the last two or three years, but the yard had definitely been neglected. The lawn was overgrown, although not to the jungle level. The window boxes were filled with browned, dried foliage, and the flower beds lining the walkway to the front porch hadn't been replanted in the spring. The pots on the porch made Ashley think that there had once been a lush container garden there, but now the pots held nothing but the dead remnants of plants. It was clear that the residents had been busy with something other than land-scaping lately.

Dreading the discussion she was about to have, Ashley stepped out of her car and start-ed up the walkway, admiring the herringbone pattern of the bricks despite the weeds poking between them. A hand-painted rug design decorated the boards of the porch; obviously, the Ortiz family enjoyed adding personal, DIY touches to their quaint, traditional home. She knocked on the door and waited.

When no one answered, she knocked again, then walked over to the picture window next to the door. The room was empty except for a hospital bed. Just as she was about to knock again, she heard a short bark and some whining, and the door slowly opened to reveal a Jack Russell terrier bouncing at the feet of a man, deep lines of grief etched into his face.

"Mr. Ortiz? My name is Ashley Adams. I wonder if you have a minute to talk to me about what happened at the golf club?"

Eyes full of pain considered her for what seemed like forever before Javier Ortiz stepped back to open the door wider. "Please come in, Ms. Adams. I don't know anything about what happened, but you look pretty determined. I'd bet that, if I don't talk to you now, you'll keep coming back until I do." He turned and walked away, clearly expecting her to follow.

"We'll go into the kitchen; we can be comfortable in there. Would you like something to drink?" He didn't seem bothered by Ashley's presence, but he appeared unable to summon enough energy to care whether she followed or not.

"A glass of water would be fine," Ashley answered, thinking that it would give him something to do while they talked. "Tap is fine; don't go to any trouble."

Ortiz took a pretty blue glass from the neatly organized cabinet and filled it with ice and water before handing it to Ashley. He picked up a *World's Best Dad* mug from the table and refilled it from a bottle on the counter. Noticing Ashley's glance, he chuckled mirthlessly and said, "It's not booze, although I've dived into a bottle or two lately. This is an herbal concoction my wife swears by for good health, although it tastes vile. Please, have a seat at the table and tell me what brings you to my home."

Ashley had been looking at the family photos on the breakfast bar; most of them pictured a cute young girl with beautiful black hair and twinkling brown eyes. In a few of the shots, the girl looked much thinner and paler, but the joy in her eyes still elicited a smile from those who saw it. Before Ashley could sit or ask any questions, he said, "That is my daughter, Gloria. She's—" He choked for a moment. "She *was* 10 years old. She died six weeks ago from cancer."

"I'm so sorry, Mr. Ortiz," Ashley said. "It's so hard to think of young children being that sick. I'm very sorry for your loss."

"Please, call me Javier," he replied. "It's a cliché, but it's true—no parent should ever outlive his children. She was definitely a daddy's girl—my angel—and there is a hole in my heart and my life that nothing else will ever fill."

Ashley hesitated for a moment, knowing her next questions were only going to add to his pain, but she knew that she had to ask if they were going to be able to help Charlie.

"Mr. Ortiz—Javier—I'm sorry to bother you now, but I believe an innocent man is being blamed for Oliver Green's murder. Can you tell me what you know about what happened that day?"

"Actually, most of what I know is what others have told me. You may have heard that I left the club early that day. In fact, I slipped out often during the last months of my daughter's life. The day of the tournament was supposed to be my first full day back. I know that two golfers found that man dead on the greens and that the sheriff's office thinks Charles Brady killed him." The venom in his voice when he said "that man" surprised Ashley.

"Did you know Dr. Green?" Ashley wondered if Ortiz would admit to being on the clinical trial participants list.

"Oh, yeah, I knew him, and I won't even pretend that I'm sorry he's dead. He only got what he deserved, and I'd like to congratulate whoever did it!" His eyes flashed with anger and bitterness. "I've never hated anyone before; I always try to find something positive in everyone I meet, but I will always hate that man with everything in me."

"He convinced my wife and me to enter Gloria into his drug trials. He promised that it would save her, making it sound like a sure thing. We were desperate, you see. None of the other treatments had been effective, and the doctors told us it was time to bring her home, make her as comfortable as possible, and wait for the end. Green insisted that his drug would do what nothing else had, that Gloria's cancer would be cured and she would become healthy again. Instead, not only did it not cure her, the side effects were horrible. That "miracle drug" of his made her suffer more than the cancer did, and then she died anyway. He was a liar who didn't care about the people he hurt." He broke down and sobbed. Ashley found a box of tissues on a nearby china cabinet and handed them to him, waiting until he calmed before speaking again.

"I'm sorry. It's so hard. I think I have my emotions under control, but I get angry all over again every time I think about what that man did to my family. We would have lost our daughter anyway, but it hurts so much to think that she went through so much suffering because I let that man persuade me to try that drug."

"Javier, it isn't your fault. You did what any parent would do—you tried everything possible to help your child. But didn't Dr. Green or his staff explain the side effects to you, at all?" Ashley had to ask.

"Wendy Graham mentioned that the drug had some unpleasant side effects, but Green waved off what she was trying to tell us and sent her away. Then he told us that the effects were minimal and asked if it wouldn't be worth a little bit of sickness or minor pain—he emphasized the word when he said it—to save Gloria's life. He *knew* what he was saying was a lie -- he *knew*!" Anger flashed across Ortiz's face again, and his hands tightened into fists.

"Did you ever talk to him about it all?" Ashley asked.

He dropped his head, looking slightly ashamed. "I was going to confront him at the tournament. I even went out on the course to find him and tell him all of what I thought of him. I found him on the seventh hole, but there was already someone with him, so I left without speaking to him."

"Was he with Charlie Brady? They were golfing partners that day," Charlie said he had left Green at the sixth hole.

"No. It was one of the volunteers. They were arguing pretty loudly, although I couldn't understand what they were saying. I didn't see Mr. Brady anywhere."

"Who was the man? Did you recognize him?" Ashley perked up; this was the first they'd heard of someone else being in the area at the time of the murder. Maybe she'd finally found a viable lead.

"No, I didn't know him. In fact, I didn't even see his face clearly; he was wearing this goofy, droopy straw hat. I know he was driving around in a golf cart, though. I think there were signs about the fundraiser still in the back of the cart; that's what they looked like, anyway." Ortiz shrugged.

Pausing for a moment to consider what she'd heard, Ashley finally asked, "Javier, the bartender told me that your boss sent you home because you were so upset and that you left the club not long before the time the detectives think Green was killed. Where did you go?"

His eyes filled with tears again. "I went to the cemetery, to Gloria's grave. I wanted to tell her again how sorry I am for putting her through the trial and to promise her that I would confront Green soon. And, before you ask, yes, someone did see me. The gatekeeper can tell you when I arrived and when I left; we've gotten to know each other since my daughter died."

Convinced that Javier Ortiz was a grieving father and not a cold-hearted murderer, Ashley thanked him for his time. As they walked to the door, he said, "Ms. Adams, I hated Oliver Green with everything in me, and his death doesn't make me sad in the least. But I don't believe for one minute that Mr. Brady had anything to do with it, and I'd hate to see him punished for someone else's crime. Please, please—if there is anything my wife or I can do for him, let us know."

"Thank you, Javier. I know that Charlie and his nephew, Ryan, will appreciate your faith in him. If you remember or hear anything that might be relevant, would you call me?" Ashley handed him a business card with her contact information. He agreed, and they shook hands.

She walked to her car and texted Ryan. *Not Ortiz—will tell U ltr. Anything new?*

Not yet—have an idea. Meet at club in a couple of hours?

After dashing off a quick agreement, Ashley stopped at the grocery store on her way to pick up a few things for a new recipe she wanted to try. After gathering fresh mint and chocolate for cookies and spinach, mushrooms, bleu cheese and eggs for a frittata, as well as a pint of Banana Split ice cream on the way, she was checking out when a deep voice behind her spoke.

"Good afternoon, Ms. Adams." It was Detective Luna.

"Detective Luna, hello," she replied. Apparently he was into healthy eating, as his cart was filled with fresh tatume and yellow squash, grape tomatoes, grapes, apples, and oranges, along with a package of skinless, boneless chicken breasts and a small loaf of whole-wheat bread. She felt a little embarrassed by her less-than-healthy groceries.

"How are things going?" he asked. "It looks like you have some baking planned."

"Yes, I'm trying a couple of new recipes for the catering business." She hesitated before continuing. "Detective, I know you can't tell me anything about your murder investigation, but Ryan and I have learned a bit more."

"Really? And what might that be?" He sounded interested, not sarcastic, so Ashley went on.

"I talked to Wendy Graham. She explained that she was not having an affair with Dr. Green. She said that the texts Jordan Berg saw were about problems with the results of their research and that Green was insisting that they report it to the FDA, while she wanted to wait until they were sure of what was going on. I also talked to Javier Ortiz, the club manager. At first, I thought he might have killed Dr. Green because of the lies the scientist told him to get him to sign on for his daughter to be a part of the clinical trials, but I don't think that happened. He was grieving, not threatening. He did tell me, though, that he saw Green arguing with one of the volunteers around the time of the murder. Charlie Brady also told us that, when he and Green were at the fifth hole, his flask of Scotch was nearly empty; when he got back to the bar, however, I remember that it was so full that it spilled when he tried to drink from it."

"Hmm. That is interesting, but I still don't see that it clears Mr. Brady. I will talk with Dr. Graham and Mr. Ortiz, but don't get your hopes up too high. Mr. Brady is still a strong suspect, although I'll admit that he isn't the only one on the list anymore."

"Thank you, Detective. I really don't expect you to take my word or Ryan's that Charlie didn't kill Dr. Green. We both understand that you have to do your job and that it includes investigating Charlie. We appreciate your open mind, though; when Ryan talked to the deputies on the scene and the day after the murder, he didn't get the idea that they were even considering that someone else might have done it."

Detective Luna looked uncomfortable at the criticism of his fellow deputies, but he acknowledged her concerns. "I know it can seem that way, especially since we can't tell you anything about our case. But I can assure you neither Sheriff Mueller nor I want to put an innocent man in prison. If Mr. Brady didn't kill Dr. Green, we'll find out who did; we aren't going to stop investigating until we are completely sure we have the right person in custody. In the meantime, I'll say it again: please be very careful about asking questions. You don't want to irritate the wrong person."

Ashley nodded and turned to pay the cashier for her groceries. "Thank you again, Detective Luna. Have a nice evening. We'll be in touch if anything else turns up."

Driving home, Ashley thought about the recipes she wanted to work on that evening, hoping that the distraction would help her sort through all she and Ryan had learned so far. She had the sense that she knew everything she needed to solve the murder, but she couldn't quite put her finger on the last piece of the puzzle. She noticed that the clouds were blackening and that the wind was picking up.

The dark weather seemed to match her mood.

In fact, thunder rumbled in the distance as she pulled into the drive. "Oh, great. Perfect timing—the storm will probably kill the power as soon as I put everything into the oven!" The area was notorious for power outages with even the weakest thunderstorm. As she opened the front door, the sky lit up with a huge lightning strike and an almost painfully loud clap of thunder.

"Whew, that was close!" she exclaimed. "It looks like I got here just in time." Just then, a hard, driving rain began to fall; before she even finished picking up her bags from the porch, where she'd placed them to unlock the front door, the water was running down the sidewalks toward the street drains.

Piling the grocery bags on the countertop, Ashley stroked her anxious dog for a moment. "Diz, it could be a long night. I know you don't like storms, but I'm afraid we've got a good one on the way. Let's get the candles ready, and you can have your supper before I start cooking. Maybe I can finish at least one recipe before the power goes out, and we have to snuggle down to wait for it to come back."

She reached to the storage cabinet above the refrigerator and retrieved a box of utility candles, several disposable aluminum mini pie pans, and some matches. Setting them on the kitchen island, she filled the dog's food bowl and freshened up her water dish. She began gathering cream, scallions, and butter for the frittata recipe she wanted to try first. As she pulled those ingredients from the refrigerator and took her purchases from the bags on the counter, she thought about her meeting with Detective Luna.

"You know," she said to Dizzy, "I don't think he paid one bit of attention to anything I had to say. All he could say was, 'I don't see how that helps clear Mr. Brady.' It's like he didn't hear a single word! I know I'm not a professional investigator, but that doesn't mean I don't have anything useful to offer!" She fumed as she recited her recipe to the pup.

"Half a cup of dairy for every large egg, Dizzy; that's the perfect ratio. Beat them with a pinch of salt until they are frothy. I don't want a quiche, with a crust, but I would like them to be bite-sized finger foods. Let's try baking them in mini muffin tins—what do you think, Dizzy doll?"

She laughed at Dizzy's excited bark. She heated some butter in a skillet while she chopped the scallions, then scooped them, along with a clove of minced garlic, into the melted butter. While that was cooking, she beat two large eggs and a cup of rich cream and sprayed the insides of the baking tin.

"Tonight's batch will be our supper, girl," she told Dizzy. "They'll have spinach and portabellas tonight, along with some crumbled bleu cheese." After slicing the mushrooms, she stacked the baby spinach and rolled the leaves to chiffonade them into ribbons. "That will give us an option for customers who don't want bacon, ham or sausage." She added the mushrooms to the onion mixture and stirred them around to coat them with butter.

"This case is making me crazy. It seems like we've eliminated all the suspects except Charlie, and I know he's innocent. I can't explain it, Dizzy; I guess it's intuition, but I just know he didn't kill anyone. And I know that I've heard something important that I've forgotten, but I can't figure out what it is or who said it."

She scattered the shredded spinach leaves in with the scallions and mushrooms and waited for them to wilt before dumping the whole mixture into the eggs, crumbling in the cheese, and stirring it all well. Then she filled each mini muffin tin and then set them on baking sheets to catch any drips before popping them into the oven.

"Okay, girl, they need about 35 minutes at

350 degrees, so let's work on dessert," she said. "I'm thinking about adding some mint leaves and orange zest to the honey sugar cookies. What do you think?" Dizzy yipped her agreement and wagged her tail.

While she waited for the stick of butter to soften, she continued talking about the case. "This whole thing is so confusing. Charlie disappeared from the course, but he can't remember why. Jordan Berg definitely had a motive—he blamed Dr. Green for the problems with his fiancée—but he has an alibi. I haven't checked with the florist, but Wendy confirmed it, and I don't think she'd lie for him because she was pretty upset with him. And she had the opportunity, since she was at the club, but she really doesn't have a motive. Killing him may have stopped Green from reporting the data problems to the FDA, but it also didn't keep it secret, and she didn't really try to hide it from us. Javier Ortiz definitely had both motive and opportunity, but something just tells me that he didn't do it. I guess I can see that, from Detective Luna's perspective, all we've done is to eliminate everyone but Charlie. To be fair—although I'm not sure I really want to be fair yet — he did let me tell him everything without interrupting, and he didn't throw out snarky attitude like he could have done. Diz, there has to be something we're missing; there has to be another suspect we haven't thought of yet."

While she was thinking, she'd creamed the butter with a quarter cup of sugar and half a cup of honey, then mixed in a cup and a half cup of flour, a quarter teaspoon of baking soda, an eighth teaspoon of salt, and a teaspoon each of chopped mint leaves and fresh orange zest. Then she wrapped the dough and set it into the refrigerator to chill for ten minutes. She poured herself a glass of iced tea, added a sprig of leftover mint, and moved to the living room couch to wait.

"And, if this murder case isn't mystery

enough, what's going on with Patty? She barely even knew we were there at dinner. Dizzy, I don't know what to do about her. I want to find out what she's thinking, but I'm afraid that asking her will start a conversation that will cost me her friendship. I wouldn't have gotten through all that mess with Serge if Patty hadn't been there for me; I don't want to lose her as my friend or my business partner. But I can't work with her if I'm walking on eggshells because I think she's mad at me. What should I do, girl?" Warm brown eyes, seemingly filled with understanding, gazed up at Ashley. Standing up to place both front paws in Ashley's lap, Dizzy nuzzled her mistress's chin with her nose, then patted Ashley's cheek with her paw. Outside, the storm rumbled on, lightning making the sky noon-bright as the rain poured down. Dizzy spun around and began barking, her body trembling.

"Ssh, girl," Ashley comforted. "It's okay; I'm

with you, and I won't let anything hurt you." She held her dog close, returning the comfort Dizzy had given her, and they cuddled together as the storm passed over them. The lights flickered several times, but they didn't go off completely. For tonight, anyway, they wouldn't need the candles after all.

As the rain slacked off and the thunder moved away into the distance, Ashley sighed. "I guess this case and relationships both are a lot like creating new recipes. You try one combination and, if it doesn't work, you keep what was good and try something else for the part that was bad. Speaking of recipes, those frittatas should be done; let's see if they turned out properly or not. I'll get the cookies into the oven while we eat."

She pulled the tins out of the oven and set them aside to cool slightly while she used her mini ice cream scoop to form perfect little cookie balls. She rolled the balls in sugar, placed them on her parchment-lined cookie sheets and flattened them. "There. Sixteen minutes at 300 degrees, and we'll have our dessert."

She picked up the first mini frittata and took a taste. "Mmmm. These are perfect. The creamy eggs work wonderfully with the sharp cheese and the veggies, and they will look great, all golden brown, on the tiered trays. Patty's going to love these! And they'll go perfectly with a light soup for luncheons or afternoon tea; maybe a vegetarian version of Italian wedding soup? Or gnocchi in vegetable broth with kale and carrots? I'll bet they'd be good with a quinoa-farro salad, too."

A few minutes later, when the cookies were out of the oven and on the cooling rack, she had another idea. Quickly, she texted Ryan. *"Need a new perspective on case—let's go to crime scene and look around."*

"Sure—last appointment should be done by 3 tomorrow; meet at the club about 3:15. Bring cookies."

Ashley laughed and sent her agreement. She put a few of the cookies in a bag to take with her the next day, then had another brainstorm. She used her mini scoop to add mint chocolate chip ice cream between two of the slightly warm cookies and tasted the sandwich.

"Oh, yeah—Patty will love the eggs, but Ryan's going to be crazy about this dessert. As he would say, 'SCORE!' C'mon, Dizzy girl, let's get some sleep. Tomorrow will be a long day."

CHAPTER 15

Ashley ran by her cottage and picked up Dizzy and a couple of bottles of water before her meeting with Ryan at the golf club. She wasn't sure if Dizzy was actually allowed on the greens, but she decided to take the chance. After all, Dizzy's abilities had come in handy before, so maybe she would find a hidden clue. Besides, it would give the pooch a change of scenery from the flower-filled backyard. Ashley hadn't had a chance to take Dizzy to the park since before the murder, and they both needed a longer walk than they'd had lately. As they climbed into the car, she looked back at her cottage and smiled at the welcoming porch with its ornate gingerbread, carved railings, lush hanging baskets, and warm red front door.

"Come on, Diz—let's find Ryan," she said as they pulled into the nearly empty parking lot. Apparently, club members didn't play much golf in the late afternoon or evening, and it was too early for the cocktails-and-dinner crowd.

Ryan was waiting for them just outside the door. "We can probably get into the bar or dining area on Uncle Charlie's name and membership, but I don't think Dizzy can pass as a member's dinner guest. Why don't we walk around the outside, through the gardens, to and bypass all the potential hassles and get to the golf course?"

"Sounds good," Ashley replied. "Besides, maybe the killer walked that way, too, and we'll find something."

As they walked along, Ashley told Ryan

about of Javier Ortiz. "He is angry, but I don't think it's killing anger. He's grieving, and I think he's angry at the universe for his daughter's death; he's focusing that anger on Green because he needs someone to blame, but I don't think he is angry enough at him to do anything more than yell. I don't think he has even had the energy for much more than that. I have to say, though, that I could understand if he did want to kill the man—not condone it, mind you—but definitely understand. Green made such big promises, and he totally misled them about the side effects of the treatment. He had to know what that little girl would go through, and he didn't care; he lied just to get them to agree to participate. And even then it didn't change the result the doctors had already said was coming. She still died."

Ryan nodded. "I talked to some of the other people on the trials list. They all said that Green blew off concerns about that sort of thing. And they said that the side effects were really bad; worse even for some than traditional chemotherapy and radiation treatments. Of course, patients who had good results from the trials think it was worth it, but even they felt strongly about the fact that Green lied to them. Still, like you said about Ortiz, no one seemed angry enough to kill over it. I think some of them might have considered suing him, but they all said that Wendy Graham's attitude and concern through everything made them decide to let it go."

The crime scene tape at the seventh hole had been taken down, but they could see where many feet had trampled what had been pristine greens. The body itself had been found at the edge of a small grove of trees, where thick underbrush covered the ground. It didn't look like the grounds crew had been there yet; the grass needed a trim, and the weeds under the bushes were beginning to encroach into the normally perfect carpet grass.

"I'll look over here by the trees," Ryan said.

"Why don't you look around on the green itself? I'm not sure what we're even looking for, but let's hope we find it anyway."

Ashley agreed, but wanted to finish telling him about her visit with the club manager. "Ortiz said that he came out here to confront Green, but one of the volunteers was with him. He said they were arguing pretty heatedly, so he walked away. Something about what he said reminded me of something, but I couldn't quite pull it out. Maybe I'll spot a clue to what's teasing my memory."

After a few minutes, Ryan called out, "Hey, Ash—there are tire tracks over here, just outside the trees. They look like they're from a golf cart. Come take a look."

"You're right," she said. "But does that mean that the killer was in a cart? Or could it just be from someone else playing the course? Do you know when the sheriff released the scene and let club members start playing again?"

He shook his head. "I'm not sure, but I don't think they took very long to finish up out here. I don't think they kept it off limits more than a day. So yeah, it doesn't necessarily mean the killer left the tracks." He looked discouraged.

"Still, it *could* have been the killer. Remember, Ortiz said he saw a golf cart here that day, and the guy Green was arguing with had been driving around the tournament that morning."

It didn't seem to cheer him up. "I don't think there's anything here for us to find, Ash," Ryan replied. "Let's go grab something to eat and figure out what to do next."

Ashley agreed and called to Dizzy, who had been sniffing through the underbrush and barking at the squirrels fussing at them from the trees. The dog came trotting over, wagging her tail triumphantly, something held firmly in her teeth.

Ryan laughed. "I swear she looks smug,

like she knows she found something when we didn't. Sometimes, I think that she's smarter than we are and that she knows it."

"Whatcha got there, Diz?" Ashley reached down to take the object. "Ryan, look—it's a straw hat. Ortiz said that the guy he saw was wearing some kind of funny straw hat." She tried not to get too excited, but she felt that tugging at the back of her mind again; there was definitely something significant about the hat.

"It sure is funny-looking," Ryan remarked. "I'll bet it covered the guy's whole face; no way he got any sunburn that day. Do you think it belongs to the killer? Why would it still be here?"

She frowned. "I don't know. Maybe it fell off when he hit Green, and then he panicked and left without looking for it. I've seen that hat before, though; I just can't place it."

"Bring it along, and let's go find a place to eat and strategize," he said. "I have a good feeling about this; I think we're getting close to the answers we need. And I’m hungry."

Ashley laughed, "Strategize? Really? All of a sudden, you sound all secret-agent-on-a-mission! That's okay, though; I'm starving. Let's get some food and make some plans."

CHAPTER 16

"Patty, do you need a coffee refill yet?" Ashley smiled at her friend as they prepared for Patty's lunchtime catering job. "I'm pouring, if you're ready!"

"Oh, heavens, yes! I could use the whole pot this morning! Why am I always running low on energy on the days I need it most?" Patty held out a greedy hand as Ashley refilled both mugs.

"I don't know the answer, but I do know the feeling. What do you need me to do next? The Paris-Brests are in the cooler." Ashley didn't mention that she'd scooped up the leftover praline cream for a decadent breakfast. "The macaroons are in the oven, and the filling is ready when the cookies are cool enough."

"Okay, that's awesome! Can you peel and dice the potatoes? We'll mix the egg yolks and seasonings in as soon as they're tender, and then can you pipe them out for pommes duchesse? You are *so* much better with the piping bag than I am!" Patty winked at her friend

"Pfft! You just don't like making the rosettes; they don't take *that* much skill with the bag! But yeah, I'll get the potatoes started boiling. What else are you serving?" Ashley laughed at Patty's ulterior motive in complimenting her.

"We'll have grilled chicken breasts with a honey Dijon sauce, the potatoes and asparagus with a buttered crumb topping. Starters will be sweet garlic soup and a spinach, bacon and mandarin orange salad. I need to make the dressing for that one still."

Ashley's mouth began to water as her stomach grumbled its approval of the menu. "Yum! That sounds amazing. Is there prepared soup in the freezer? I can get that started thawing and fry up the bacon while the potatoes are boiling. And what's in the soup? I don't think I've had that one yet, and it sounds delicious."

"Perfect! Yes, I made up the soup last week, so we should have plenty. It's got six cloves of roasted garlic mixed with butter and flour to make a roux. When that was a pretty golden color, I added basil, thyme, rosemary, oregano, salt and pepper, and chicken stock. I was thinking about asiago croutons to top it. Anyway, once it's thawed, we can heat it up at the venue instead of trying to transport it hot." Patty looked past Ashley, and her face broke into a huge smile. "I think I'll try a new dressing recipe with orange juice, orange zest, a little mint, and olive oil. What do you think?"

"Oh, yeah! That sounds like a perfect

match for the oranges in the salad. How about a few slices of red onion in the salad, too?" Patty nodded, but she was interrupted before she could say anything.

"Good morning, ladies! And how are the most beautiful chefs in Seagrass this beautiful morning?" boomed a deep male voice. Ashley turned to see Smoke Daddy Lee coming through the back door to the kitchen, shaking water from his Stetson.

"You old fool! It's pouring rain out there," scolded Patty, still smiling. "Beautiful day, my foot!"

"Ah, darlin', anytime I wake up still breathing, it's a beautiful day, and it's even better when I get to spend time with my favorite people." Smoke Daddy's face had that aw-shucks grin that had made women forgive men for almost anything since the beginning of time.

They all laughed, and Ashley asked, "What brings you out to our kitchens on a wet summer morning?"

"I invited him to come down and help get things ready for the luncheon. I figured we could use the extra hands for carrying food to the van and into the hall, if not before then." Ashley thought that seemed a little odd, especially when she noticed that Patty was blushing as she looked down at the bowl of sauce she was mixing.

"So, put me to work, ladies. What do you need me to do first?" Smoke Daddy winked at Patty, making her blush even more.

"Why don't you mix up a batch of your yeast rolls? Those would be the perfect finish to our menu," Patty answered. "Then, maybe you could wash the spinach and finish up the salad?"

Smoke Daddy nodded and picked up a large mixing bowl, carrying it with him for gathering flour, yeast, and the other ingredients for his "top secret" roll recipe. He seemed to know his way around their kitchen surprisingly well without having to ask where to find things.

They all worked together for the next couple of hours, sharing funny stories about restaurant and catering fiascos.

Patty said, "My favorite bad memory was when I was a personal chef for a young couple and their two toddlers; it taught me to never serve a new recipe until I had tried it myself. I'd been reading recipes for authentic Mexican food, and I decided that I would use a little chili in a chocolate dessert. I added some dried jalapeño powder to the cake batter, and then I made a pudding-type of filling for between the layers. I added a quarter teaspoon of cayenne powder to that. So far, everything would probably have been fine, but I decided that no one would be able to taste the peppers, so I added more jalapeño powder to the frosting and topped it with candied jalapeño slices. I've had hot wings that didn't have as much heat as that cake. For six weeks after that, even setting a spice jar with pepper in it on the counter to get to something behind it made the family crave a take-out meal!"

Ashley giggled and said, "I think you've got me beat with that one. The worst I ever did was when I left the flour out of the groom's cake for 500 wedding guests. Fortunately, I had several batches of brownies in the freezer; I used the cake frosting on top of them, cut them into triangles instead of rectangles, and topped them with walnut halves. Only the bride, her mother, and I knew we weren't serving what we had planned, and they thought the whole thing was funny. Besides, they heard so many compliments about how fancy the "cake" pieces looked that they weren't about to let anyone else in on the secret!"

More laughter; then Smoke Daddy asked, "Do y'all remember Bertha Mae? She worked for me from the first day we opened—or rather, she let me work there and bossed me and everyone else, including the customers. Anyway, one day, a young woman came in with her boyfriend; it didn't take long to figure out that she wasn't from Texas. Bertha Mae took water and menus to the table, where the young man told her that everyone they'd talked to since they came to town had told them to eat barbecue at Smoke Daddy Lee's place. The young lady claimed that they couldn't wait for their barbecue plates. Bertha Mae asked if they wanted brisket, sausage, or ribs, or if they'd like sampler plates. The girl looked at her in horror and announced that she didn't eat meat, fat, or sugar. Shaking her head, Bertha Mae suggested a turnip greens, pinto bean, and grilled corn vegetable plate with a side salad and cornbread, but that wasn't going to do it! Nope—that one insisted she wanted barbecue, but with no meat. The boyfriend broke in and suggested a chicken plate, hold the chicken, and the girl agreed—with pinto beans, grilled corn and turnip greens as her sides."

He held up his hand. "Wait—that's not the

best part. When Bertha Mae brought their food to the table, the girl wanted to know where the butter for her corn and bread was, and then decided she wanted some pecan cobbler because 'that would be a healthy dessert, with all those nuts.' I heard Bertha Mae say, 'Bless your heart, girlie,' and I headed to the back of the kitchen as fast as I could. I never found out what else she said to the girl, but the boyfriend left the biggest tip Bertha Mae or any of the other waitresses had ever seen."

When they could stop laughing enough to breathe again, Ashley washed up the dishes they'd used, while Smoke Daddy and Patty loaded up the food into the van. She'd turned to say something to Patty when she saw them exchange a tender glance; suddenly, everything from the last few weeks made sense.

"Hey, you two! How long have you been an item? And why didn't you tell me?" Ashley put her hands on her hips in an attempt to look angry, but the sparkle in her eyes gave her away. She couldn't think of anyone better suited than those two, once she considered it for a second.

"Girl, you know this place; if we told anyone, it would be all over town within ten minutes! We just wanted the chance to get to know each other and enjoy some time together without being the object of everyone's gossip obsession!" Patty looked worried that her friend might really be upset with her.

Shaking her head, Ashley said, "Yeah, I guess I can understand that. But I have to admit, I thought you were mad at me or something, because you didn't seem to want to spend any time together lately. I thought you didn't approve of my taking business time to go sleuthing with Ryan."

Smoke Daddy's laugh filled the commercial kitchen; Ashley was almost willing to swear that the pots on the shelves were rattling from his guffaws. "Darlin', I told you to tell her!

Ashley, hon, not only does she approve of your sleuthing, she's been going crazy because she wasn't helping out. She kept telling me about what you found out and making lists and charts with the information. I finally had to hide the paper and pencils at my place so she'd spend a little time talking to me when we were together! Not approve—that's too funny!"

Patty waited, pretending to be impatient, until the others had stopped laughing, then shook her head. "I didn't want to butt in; you and Ryan seemed to finally be spending some time together, and I didn't want to mess that up. I know he had a big crush on you before, and it sure seemed like you might be getting interested in him lately. No way was I going to interfere with that! And I'm sorry about not spending time together; Lee and I have been working around our crazy schedules to find time to be together."

"I was so worried that you thought I wasn't

taking the business seriously enough. You've been so supportive since I decided to start it, and I didn't want you to think it wasn't important to me. I definitely still need your advice, and I was so scared I'd messed up both our friendship and your willingness to help me."

The two friends hugged each other, and Ashley knew things were good between them again. To lighten things up, she asked Smoke Daddy, "How did you get started in the barbecue business? And what was the most important tip you got when you were starting out?"

"Well, the restaurant was kind of an accident. My sister decided I needed to take charge of cooking the meats for a big family reunion—never mind that I had never cooked anything more complicated than a TV dinner in my life. She announced that we were having brisket and sausage and that I was doing the barbecuing. Next thing I knew, friends and family were asking me to cook for their parties, church events and fundraisers. About the time I realized that I was having fun doing it, my sister came to my house with another announcement: my new barbecue joint was opening in two weeks, and I'd better get busy on finding the right building and suppliers, because she'd already put an ad in the newspaper and stuck posters up all over town. Twenty years later, she still walks in to inform me that she's hired someone to work in the place, that I'm redecorating and how, or that something is being added or removed from the menu. She's a force of nature, and I don't even try to argue with her anymore!" They all laughed, knowing his sister well enough to know that he wasn't exaggerating much at all.

"As for business advice, I think the best suggestion was that you should name your business after yourself and then hang out a big sign for everyone to see. When you put your name out there where people can see it, they start to believe that you really can make what you promise happen."

Ashley's head jerked up at his words. "Oh, my gosh! That's it! Patty, do you need me at the luncheon? Can you manage without me there?" She was already pulling off her apron and heading for her purse under the front counter as she asked.

"Lee's helping, and I have several college students meeting us there to do the actual serving, so we're good. Are you okay, though?" Patty looked concerned. "Where are you going?"

"Yes, I just realized who the killer is. I have to go somewhere; I'll call you later." Ashley grabbed her purse and rushed toward her car.

"Ashley! Don't go confronting a killer by yourself!" She heard Patty call out to her as the door closed behind her. It was pretty good advice, though, so she texted Ryan on her way out. "*Figured it out. Meet me at the kitchens, we need to go to the lab!*"

His response was immediate, as if he'd been staring at his phone and waiting for her text. *"Be there in 10. Call Luna and wait outside for me."*

CHAPTER 17

When Ryan arrived in front of the kitchen building, Ashley opened his passenger door while the car was still rolling and jumped into the seat.

"Detective Luna said to meet him in the parking lot nearest to the lab building. He doesn't want us to confront anyone until he gets there and until we catch him up on what we've learned," she reported. "Thank goodness you had already told the sheriff about some of it."

"Makes sense. But you said you know who the killer is? Who is it, Ash?"

"I'd rather wait until we get there; I'm still not 100% sure—more like 95%," she teased. "I don't want to say anything until I check out one more thing. But, if I'm right, we owe Smoke Daddy Lee big time; it was one of his business tips that made things click for me."

Traffic was light, so it only took about thirty minutes to get to the campus and navigate to the science lab, but it felt more like thirty hours to them. As they pulled into the nearly empty lot, Ashley pointed out the detective's car.

"That has to be him," she said. "Nobody else would be sitting in a closed car, without the engine and A/C running, in this heat and humidity. And nobody but plainclothes cops drive that kind of nondescript sedan. I guess he didn't want to take the chance someone in the lab would see him and run if he drove the department's new decaled SUV." Ashley and Ryan got out of the car and walked over as the detective emerged from his car.

They went into the building next to the lab, where there was a small coffee bar and a few small tables and chairs. They chose the table farthest from the barista and began talking about what the friends had learned.

"Okay. Ms. Adams, you say that the club manager saw someone arguing with the victim not long before the murder?" Detective Luna asked. "And, Mr. Bregar, you checked your uncle's phone records and found out he got a call just before that?"

"Yes," Ashley said. "And Javier didn't mention seeing Charlie around while the two men were arguing. I think he would have said something if he'd seen all three of them, instead of just Dr. Green and the mystery guy. He was pretty surprised that y'all even suspected Charlie, so—"

The detective nodded to indicate he understood her point.

"Yes, and we found out that Jordan Berg and Javier Ortiz had motives to want Dr.

Green dead," Ryan contributed, "but they can account for their time that day. Wendy Graham wasn't having an affair with Green, after all, and his death wouldn't have done their research or her career any good, so I don't think she killed him, either."

Ashley took up the narrative. "Blake Simmons and Evan Richards both had reasons to get rid of him, though. Blake said he was here that morning and then left to go surfing, but I didn't check to see if he was telling the truth, and we never asked Evan where he was."

"Why are you sure there was no affair?" the detective asked. "I don't think you can just take her word for it, in light of the emails her fiancé found. It still sounds like Green was threatening to tell Berg about his relationship with Ms. Graham."

"That's what was bothering me about the messages," Ashley suddenly realized. "Dr. Green said that he and Wendy had to tell 'them,' not 'him.' The only person who would have been invested in knowing about them was Jordan Berg—not a 'them' at all. He *was* talking about the FDA and their data! That's why I believed her before, when I told you about it in the grocery store. I couldn't figure it out then, but I knew I'd heard something that made me believe her."

"All right," Luna said. "You two wait here; I'll go talk to those guys and see what they have to say."

"Detective, I don't think they'll tell you anything, but I believe I can get some information from them. What if Ryan and I go to the lab, and you follow us and wait in the adjoining classroom? You can hear everything we all say, and you can come in at the right time to make an arrest, if we get the right clues." Ashley looked up at the detective, surreptitiously crossing her fingers and hoping that he'd go along with the plan.

"Absolutely not! There's no way I'm letting a couple of civilians get in the middle of this.

The coroner said that whoever hit Green was in a rage; if the killer is in there and figures out that you're on to him, it could be dangerous for you. I'll handle it. If I can't get them to talk, I'll take all of them back to the station and keep them until they decide to tell me what they know."

Detective Luna's eyes held a don't-mess-with-me look, and Ashley had a short moment of panic; everything was going to fall apart. She was certain the killer was cool enough to maintain the façade of innocence in front of law enforcement personnel, but he might more likely brag to someone he viewed as being below his intelligence level, a "mere" female caterer without any background in science or academia. He didn't know her background and training, and she thought they should take advantage of his ignorance.

Before she could speak, though, Ryan said, "Detective, you'll be all of the thickness of a door away, so you can get there if things go south. You can even keep the door cracked, so you won't have to do anything but push it open the rest of the way. From what we've learned, the murderer didn't bring a weapon with him—he used what was already close at hand. That means he probably doesn't have a gun or another weapon on him, so, even if he snaps, it should take a couple of seconds for him to find something to attack with, and you can be in there before that happens. I don't know who she thinks it is, but I think Ashley's right about him not giving anything away during an official interrogation. She's really good at getting people to tell her things they don't mean to share, though; if anyone can get him to talk, it's definitely her."

The detective hesitated a moment, ruminating, and then he nodded. "Okay, this is how we're going to do it. We go in, and I check out the setup. If I think I can protect you, we'll try it your way. If there's anything that makes me think I can't get into the room quickly, you two will come back here and wait while I talk to them. And, just so you know, I wouldn't even consider this if the sheriff hadn't told me about how you helped him clear up that poisoning case a ways back. He thought you handled yourself well, and he trusts you." Exchanging a relieved glance, Ashley and Ryan quickly agreed.

They walked to the second floor of the lab building and found the classroom next to the cancer researchers' lab. Detective Luna slipped inside, looked around at the lab tables and stools, then checked the connecting door. Apparently satisfied, he nodded at Ashley and Ryan to let them know that they could go next door and confront Blake and Evan.

As they approached the open lab door, Wendy, Blake, and Evan could be heard discussing how to divide up the tasks that Green's death left undone. The three scientists looked up, startled, as Ashley and Ryan entered without knocking. Ashley noticed the connecting door opening the tiniest bit; Luna was obviously using their entrance to cover any sound the door might make.

"Hello," Wendy said, looking surprised. "What are you doing here?" She flushed at her own rudeness. "I'm sorry; I didn't mean to be impolite. Is there something you need, though?"

"Hi, Wendy," Ashley replied. "This is Ryan Bregar; he is Charlie Brady's nephew. We had a couple of questions about Dr. Green's death that we were hoping y'all could help us with."

"We don't have time for you and your snoopy questions," Evan growled. "We have things to do that are actually important." Ashley knew then that she hadn't overestimated his arrogance; she still wasn't sure about Blake, but she thought she could definitely get Evan to talk more than he should.

"Evan! There's no need for that," Wendy exclaimed as Blake looked on, seemingly astonished at his colleague's nastiness. "It won't hurt to take a few minutes to talk with them."

"More important than the death of your boss?" Ashley asked, ignoring the other woman's attempt to smooth things over. "Maybe like getting your paper published?"

"As a matter of fact..." Evan didn't bother to hide the disdain in his voice.

Ashley interrupted before he could continue. "This won't take long, and it could have a pretty significant impact on the future of this project and the journal article. And I'm very sure that your colleagues—and the police, of course—will find what we've learned to be far more important than a research paper, even one about a lifesaving drug."

Evan started to brush her off again, but Blake stopped him. "What are you talking about? How could your questions affect our paper? And what do you know that is so important?" Ashley looked closely at him, trying to decide if he was nervous or just curious.

"I'd like to know that, too," Wendy said, beginning to look annoyed. "Oliver's death means the rest of us have to do some extra work to finish his portion of the project, but the only real impact will be that it takes a little longer to get the manuscript ready to send to the journal for review and publication. I'm sorry, Ms. Adams, but your statement does seem a bit melodramatic, don't you think?"

"What if one of you is arrested for murder? Wouldn't that make a difference?" Ryan shot back. Blake and Wendy stared at him, open-mouthed, while Evan narrowed his eyes and glared at Ashley.

"What? What are you talking about?" Wendy sounded shocked, and her surprise seemed sincere.

"Don't be ridiculous," Evan sneered. "Even if one of us killed him—and we didn't—what could *you* possibly know about it? You're a cook, not a cop."

"Evan, you were at the golf tournament the

day Dr. Green was killed, weren't you?" Ashley asked.

"Yeah, so what? The money was going to pay for the rest of our research, so I figured I ought to do my part to help out. It's stupid, but you have to schmooze with the money people; wastes a lot of time, but you have to suck up, sometimes. I was just doing my part." His tone hadn't improved; clearly, he thought they were too stupid to realize they were wasting their time.

"Blake, you were here at the lab that day; isn't that what you told me?" Ashley turned to the intern.

"Sure. Dr. Green thought someone should be here; he wanted someone at the lab 24/7, and I volunteered to stay. I don't play golf, and I'm not all that into the great outdoors. Dr. Green, Dr. Graham and Evan are better with the donors and people like that, anyway; I don't feel comfortable with people with a lot of money to throw around."

"Was there anyone else here with you that day?"

"No, I was here alone. Well, I was here by myself most of the day. There were a few people around for a little while in the morning, but then everyone left for the fundraiser." Blake looked puzzled. "Even most of the interns took the day off. I stayed around until around noon, until one of them came back, and then I took off for Corpus to catch some waves."

"I thought you said this wouldn't take long," Evan snarled. "What's your point? That Blakey was alone, so he could have slipped out and popped Dr. Green on the head without anyone missing him?" The other student looked indignant, either at the snarky nickname or at his fellow student throwing him under the bus. "If so, you're way off base. He doesn't have the guts to confront anyone, much less kill them. He can't work up enough passion about anything to get that angry."

Ashley ignored him. “Blake, was Dr. Green here that morning?"

"Yes, he came by for about an hour. It's his lab, so that wasn't unusual. Why?"

"What about Evan? Did he stop by as well?" Ashley hoped she wasn't about to make a complete fool of herself.

Blake looked sideways at Evan. "Yeah, he was. I remember now that he and Dr. Green were talking in the classroom.” He pointed at the door. "I didn't hear what they were saying, but I think Dr. Green was really pi—angry." He turned toward Evan, his face showing he was beginning to understand.

Ashley turned back to Evan. "He was angry, wasn't he? He confronted you about the data manipulation you've been doing. He told you that he was going to talk to Charlie Brady about investing in the project, but then he told you that he was halting the work until the discrepancies were cleared up, and that he was dropping you from the project because your fake data jeopardized both his results and his reputation."

"That's ridiculous!" Evan snapped. "Yes, we talked; he told me he was going to ask the old sot for more money, but that's all. No one was angry, because no one changed any test results. Why would anyone do something like that?"

"Really? Wendy, didn't you tell me that you and Dr. Green had discussed the fact that the results were too good and that someone had clearly been changing them?" Wendy's face was starting to show comprehension as well. "Didn't you say that, if it was intentional, it was most likely that one of the Ph.D. candidates was responsible?"

"Yes. He wanted to tell the board and the FDA right away. I convinced him to wait until after the fundraiser, but there was no doubt that the results were wrong." Wendy looked at Evan. "He accused you of manipulating the data? You're the one who did it? How stupid are you? Do you have any idea what you've done to this project, what your actions are going to cost us and the patients who are waiting for this drug?"

Evan didn't answer. He crossed his arms over his chest. and tried to look disinterested, but his darting eyes gave him away.

"You were driving around the course, putting up signs that morning, weren't you, Evan? In fact, you almost ran over me in the parking lot because you had them piled up so high," Ashley continued. "You drove your cart out to the fifth hole to meet Charlie and Dr. Green; you knew Dr. Green was going to ask Charlie to help pay for the go-to-market campaign, and you wanted to make sure it happened without him saying anything about the data. You took a bottle of Charlie's favorite Scotch; you figured that would seal the deal. But then you heard Dr. Green tell Charlie that the money might not be needed for several months or maybe even longer because he was stopping the research to double-check on some results. You knew then that he was going to follow through with his threats to you here that morning."

She paused to gauge Evan's reaction. He still didn't speak, but he dropped his arms, clenching his fists tightly enough that his knuckles turned white, and his whole body almost vibrated with anger.

"You waited until they finished the sixth hole, then you called Charlie on his cell phone and told him there was an emergency at the clubhouse that needed his attention. You intercepted him along the way and refilled his flask, knowing his weakness. He was already pretty crocked, so you stole his phone at the same time, covering your tracks. You figured as long as the phone was missing no one would know that you made the call, and no one would believe that Charlie wasn't with Green when he was killed."

Still no reaction. She went on. "You know a

lot about science and cancer research, but you apparently don't know as much about technology, especially cell phones. Ryan was able to get copies of the call log and found a call from your number—it is 574-1029, right?"

Evan's head came up sharply. "How did you get my phone number? That's none of your business."

She ignored this too. "Once Charlie was on his way, you found Dr. Green at the seventh hole. When he wouldn't back down on stopping the project and blew you off to go back to his game, you clubbed him over the head with the mallet you were using to pound the signs into the dry ground around the course. You must have already had it planned in case you couldn't talk him into staying quiet. The wind blew your hat off, but you didn't want to take the time to look for it. You had to get away from the scene before the next golfers got there in order to blame the murder on Charlie."

Ryan spoke up. "FYI—the event photographer got lots of pictures, and CURE's publicist posted them to their Instagram account. There are several shots of you wearing that ridiculous hat. It's pretty noticeable; there couldn't be another one that silly-looking around. And the photographer did manage to catch your face under the hat in a couple of those shots, too, so there's no use denying it's yours."

"Anyway," Ashley continued, "after you dragged Dr. Green's body into the underbrush, you drove the cart to the clubhouse and returned it to the storage lot. You disabled Charlie's phone, left it where someone would find it and turn it in, and left the event. You knew the sheriff would suspect Dr. Green's golfing partner, and you knew that Charlie was probably too drunk to remember enough to incriminate you. Unfortunately for you, someone saw you arguing with Dr. Green on the seventh hole, and your hat helps prove you were there."

Evan's fists came up. "Yes, I killed him!" he shouted. "I need that publication credit. I worked my tail off in graduate school for eight years, and then I slaved for that jerk for four more. He never acknowledged my work; he didn't appreciate everything I did on this project. My name on that paper means I'll be taken seriously enough to have my pick of jobs anywhere I want to go. He was going to take that away from me, but I stopped him. He got what he had coming to him; he asked for it. He can't fire me now, can he?"

“You nosy little...“ Evan suddenly lunged at Ashley, hands outstretched toward her throat. "You're not going to ruin this for me. I'll shut you up!"

"Freeze! Get away from her, or I'll drop you now."

They all heard the click of Detective Luna's sidearm as he cocked the hammer in preparation for firing. Momentarily stunned, Ryan and Blake shook it off and grabbed Evan, wrestling him away from Ashley and to the ground so that the detective could handcuff him While the detective read him his Miranda rights. Evan twisted until he could see Ashley, hate filling his face.

"He deserved it! He was a malicious, arrogant bastard, and he was going to ruin my life. He deserved to die." He made an unsuccessful attempt to move towards her, but Luna's hand yanked him back. "If you stayed out of it, it would have all worked out—the paper would have been published, the drug would go on the market, and I'd finally get the job I've dreamed about. You ruined everything!" He continued yelling as Luna dragged him from the room and down to the car.

Trembling, Wendy dropped heavily onto a stool. When she looked up, her eyes were filled with tears. "Oliver *was* arrogant, and he had the social skills of a seashell, but he didn't deserve to die. I can't believe Evan killed him over a research paper. Oliver wouldn't have let

Evan's name go on the paper, and he wouldn't have written him a glowing recommendation, but he wouldn't have said anything about the data manipulation."

Ryan looked skeptical. "What makes you so sure? Wouldn't he have wanted to make sure Evan didn't do the same thing somewhere else?"

"If someone else asked, he wouldn't have lied about it, but he wouldn't have brought it up to begin with. We had an intern on another project who screwed up the data from the research so badly that we had to drop it all and start from the beginning—that's how we ended up on this project—and Oliver only fired him. When the guy's next potential employer called, Oliver said he worked hard as long as he had clear instructions and close supervision. He believed everyone deserves a second chance." Tears began rolling down her cheeks. "There were times I absolutely hated that man, too. I didn't think I was mourning his death at all, but I guess I was fooling myself. And I can't believe Evan still thought his name would be on the paper after he confessed to murder; did he really think that, if he got to you, Blake and I would go along with his plans?"

Just then, Jordan Berg rushed in, halting when he saw his fiancée in tears. "Wendy, baby—what's wrong?" He turned to glare at Ashley and Ryan. "What did you do to her?"

"Jordan, stop; it's not their fault. Evan just confessed to killing Oliver. Everything hit me finally; Ashley and Ryan didn't do anything. What are you doing here, anyway? I told you I needed some time away from our relationship to work things out in my mind, and yet here you are. How can I think properly if you won't even respect my request?"

He stammered for a moment, then said, "I drove over to see if you would go to lunch with me. I want to make up for the stupid things my jealousy made me do. I hope I can convince you to forgive me."

She sighed. "We have a lot to talk about, Jordan. We can't get married unless we both trust each other. And we both have to understand and accept the needs of the other." She looked at her fiancé with uncertainty in her eyes, but it looked like there was still a spark of love that left some hope for their future together.

Ashley realized that their presence was definitely no longer needed, so she signaled Ryan, who looked at Blake and jerked his head towards the door. They slipped out, leaving the couple together to begin to repair their relationship.

"Man, I can't believe that!" Blake was apparently still feeling the effects of the adrenaline rush from the confrontation. "Evan killed Oliver Green. I can't wrap my head around it; I was working with a murderer! Wait until I tell my roommate!" Still exclaiming, he rushed off.

"Ah, the enthusiasm and resilience of youth," Ashley remarked, amused. "It makes me feel old and tired just to watch him!" She slipped her arm through Ryan's and smiled at him as they returned to his car, hoping that things would work out for Wendy and Jordan—not to mention for her and Ryan.

CHAPTER 18

"Look out!" Patty shouted as she watched her golf ball leave the ground and fly through the air. She and Smoke Daddy Lee had agreed to play a round of golf with Ashley and Ryan, even though Ryan was the only one of them who had played before.

"Patty! You're putting; you aren't supposed to hit the ball hard enough to lift it up like that!" Ryan objected. "Tap it gently toward the hole—this one, not the one in the next green!"

"Hey, I told you when you invited us that I've never played golf before," Patty huffed. "I've never even watched anyone play before.

You had to know we'd be pretty bad at it!" The twinkle in her eyes defeated her attempt to look insulted.

"Yeah, what's that about, anyway?" Smoke Daddy Lee asked. "I love me some sports on the TV, but who watches televised golf? Watching the dew dry is more exciting than watching those guys squatting down to stare at their golf balls! Give me a good Spurs game over that, any day, any way!"

Ryan opened his mouth to reply and thought better of it. There really wasn't a good answer to that one; he loved playing golf, especially with Uncle Charlie, but he had to admit that it was pretty slow to be much of a spectator sport. He pretended to look miffed and bent to line up his own putt.

"So, Ash, how did you figure out that Evan was the killer?" Patty asked. "There were several other good murder suspects. I was really sure it was going to be Jordan Berg or maybe Javier Ortiz."

Ashley smiled at Smoke Daddy. "It was Smoke Daddy's business advice that clued me in. What he said about putting your name out there and making things happen with the customers; it all came together. Someone mentioned that Evan's grant was running out and he was looking for a new job. He had to get his name out there, like a business owner, and that professional paper was the key to his future. When Smoke Daddy said that, I remembered that Javier Ortiz mentioned having seen someone arguing with Dr. Green. I also remembered seeing that stupid hat when Evan almost ran me down in the parking lot. I didn't recognize him when I first went to the lab, but something kept nagging at me after we found the hat. It wasn't until I realized how much was at stake for him that the hat and the fact that he was driving around the course seemed important enough to think about. After that, when I considered what we heard about Dr. Green's ethical stance in the labs, it seemed obvious that he'd fired Evan as soon as he was sure that's where the false data came from. That meant that Evan had the three things mystery stories emphasize—motive, means, and opportunity."

"Well, I'm glad it's over," Ryan said. "Uncle Charlie's off the hook for the murder, and he's doing well in rehab. He should be home in another week or two. He's already told his lawyer to get the divorce settled, no matter what it takes. He says none of his possessions are important enough to drive him back into addiction, and that my aunt can take it all, if that's what it takes to get that stress out of his life. I think he's finally ready to move forward with his life instead of clinging to what wasn't working for them anymore."

"Relationships can be tricky," Patty said, looking innocent, "especially if they are all talk and no walk."

"Yeah, keeping secrets from your best friend definitely isn't cool," Ashley teased. She knew what Patty was hinting at, but there was no way she'd admit it in that group. She was getting impatient waiting for Ryan to plan his elaborate surprise, but she wasn't about to jinx it by talking about it with Patty and Smoke Daddy listening in. She really did wonder if she'd blown her only chance at romance with Ryan by telling too much about her past, but she had felt so comfortable talking to him that she couldn't help herself.

"Sometimes talking is overrated," Ryan remarked, not helping at all. "Sometimes you just have to go for it without thinking or talking it to death beforehand." With that, he walked off toward the next hole, leaving Ashley even more confused.

Smoke Daddy Lee roared with laughter. "That boy's pretty smart. Maybe we'll all be surprised at what comes next!"

Ashley and Patty looked at each other, wide-eyed, before they dissolved into laughter themselves. Whatever happened, they'd see it through together.

"Hey, Patty!" Ryan yelled, turning back to look at them.

"Yeah, Ryan; what do you want?"

"It's 'fore,' Patty," he hollered. "Look out, it's 'fore!'"

THE END

Letter from the Author

Thank you so much for reading. I hope you enjoyed this story and will consider writing a review on Amazon.com or lending it to a friend.

To be the first to know when the next book in the series and other new releases are out, join my email list www.SandiScottBooks.com

I love to stay in touch with readers and periodically give out free books, advanced copies, and other fun stuff.

Email me to let me know more about yourself at sandi@sandiscottbooks.com

Stay cozy,

Sandi

Apple Tarte Tatin

For more recipes from the book, visit my website

www.SandiScottBooks.com/recipes

Ingredients:

- 5 pounds firm apples (granny smith's work very well)
- 1/2 cup salted butter
- 1 1/2 cups sugar
- one sheet store bought frozen puff pastry, thawed
- 1/4 cup calvados
- 8 ounces creme fraiche

Directions:

1. Preheat oven to 375 degrees. Place a rack in the center of the oven.
2. Peel the apples. Using a melon baller and a paring knife remove the core of the apples. Trim the ends of the apples so they are flat.
3. In a 9 - 10 inch oven safe pan with straight sides, melt the butter.

4. When the butter is melted, add the sugar and stir it until it is melted and a deep golden brown. The caramel should be smooth and consistent in color.
5. Remove the caramel from the heat and allow to cool for about 5 minutes.
6. On a floured surface roll out the puff pastry dough until it is very thin and larger than the pan. Using the lid of the pan for a guide, cut the pastry into a circle which will fit over the pan.
7. When the caramel has firmed up just a bit, arrange the apples in concentric circles, standing on end into the caramel in concentric circles.
8. Cut a small circle out of the center of the dough (about the size of a dime) and rest it on top of the apples. Any excess dough can be tucked in between the apples and the side of the pan.
9. Place the pan on a baking sheet and into the oven on the center rack. Allow tarte to bake for about 45 minutes, until the crust is golden brown.

10. Remove pan from oven and place it on a burner over high heat for about 5 minutes to cook off some of the excess moisture (it will still look a little saucy).
11. Place a platter that is slightly larger than the pan and the tart over the lip of the pan. Invert the pan over the platter to release the tarte.
12. Pour the Calvados into the pan and heat it over medium heat, scraping up any bits of apple left in the pan. Spoon the heated Calvados over the tarte and allow it to cool.
13. Allow the tarte to cool for about 45 minutes. When cooled, cut it into wedges and serve it with dollops of creme fraiche.

From Foodista.com

Thanks again for reading. Connect with me online to …

- *Read the next book in the series*
- *Read recipes from this book*
- *Learn more about me*

www.SandiScottBooks.com

68267043R00142

Made in the USA
San Bernardino, CA
01 February 2018